"How about I do this?"

Name: Ryou Takamori

Age: 17

School year: high school, second year

Height: 5'9"

Self-proclaimed boring dude struggling to fit in. He's been estranged from Hina since middle school until the train incident brought them back together.

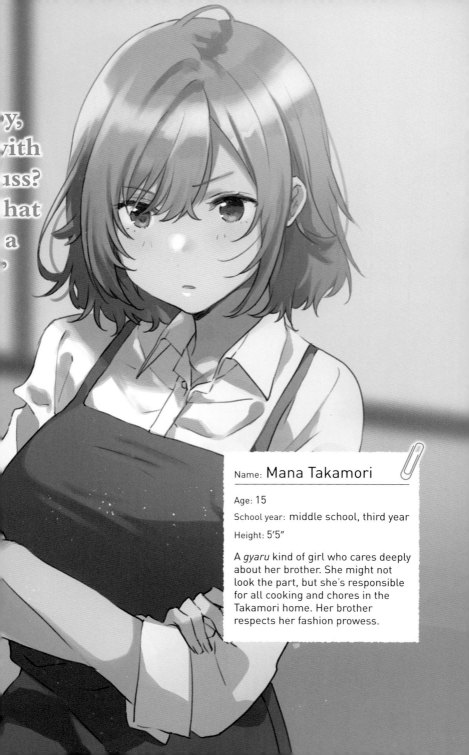

y,
ith
ss?
hat
a
,

Name: Mana Takamori

Age: 15

School year: middle school, third year

Height: 5'5"

A *gyaru* kind of girl who cares deeply about her brother. She might not look the part, but she's responsible for all cooking and chores in the Takamori home. Her brother respects her fashion prowess.

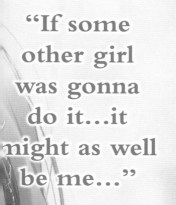

"If some other girl was gonna do it...it might as well be me..."

"Bubb what's v all the f What's t about kiss?"

Name: Shizuka Torigoe

Age: 17

School year: high school, second year

Height: 4'10"

A reserved girl who has lunch with Ryou every day in the physics room, although they sit far away from each other. She's proud of being Ryou's closest friend, understanding him at a higher level than even he himself does.

"I might get wet if we don't get closer... Is that okay?"

Name: Hina Fushimi

Age: 17

School year: high school, second year

Height: 5'3"

Ryou's childhood friend and an immensely popular, gorgeous girl. Ryou doesn't seem to notice her clear advances on him.

The Girl I Saved on the Train Turned Out to Be My Childhood Friend

Kennoji

Illustration by Fly

©Fly

The Girl I Saved on the Train Turned Out to Be My Childhood Friend

1

Kennoji

Illustration by Fly

YEN
ON

New York

The Girl I Saved on the Train Turned Out to Be My Childhood Friend ①

Kennoji

Translation by Sergio Avila
Cover art by Fly

CHIKAN SARESOU NI NATTEIRU S-KYU BISHOUJO WO TASUKETARA TONARI NO SEKI NO OSANANAJIMI DATTA volume 1
Copyright © 2020 Kennoji
Illustrations copyright © 2020 Fly
All rights reserved.
Original Japanese edition published in 2020 by SB Creative Corp.
This English edition is published by arrangement with SB Creative Corp., Tokyo in care of Tuttle-Mori Agency, Inc., Tokyo.

English translation © 2021 by Yen Press, LLC

Yen On
150 West 30th Street, 19th Floor
New York, NY 10001

Visit us at yenpress.com ✧ facebook.com/yenpress ✧ twitter.com/yenpress ✧ yenpress.tumblr.com ✧ instagram.com/yenpress

First Yen On Edition: November 2021

Yen On is an imprint of Yen Press, LLC.
The Yen On name and logo are trademarks of Yen Press, LLC.

The publisher is not responsible for websites (or their content) that are not owned by the publisher.

Library of Congress Cataloging-in-Publication Data
Names: Kennoji, author. | Fly, 1963– illustrator. | Avila, Sergio, translator.
Title: The girl I saved on the train turned out to be my childhood friend / Kennoji ;
    illustration by Fly ; translation by Sergio Avila.
Other titles: Chikan saresou ni natteiru s-kyu bishoujo wo tasuketara
    tonari no seki no osananajimi datta. English
Description: First Yen On edition. | New York, NY : Yen On, 2021.
Identifiers: LCCN 2021039082 | ISBN 9781975336998 (v. 1 ; trade paperback)
Subjects: CYAC: Love—Fiction. | LCGFT: Light novels.
Classification: LCC PZ7.1.K507 Gi 2021 | DDC [Fic]—dc23
LC record available at https://lccn.loc.gov/2021039082

ISBNs: 978-1-9753-3699-8 (paperback)
       978-1-9753-3700-1 (ebook)

10 9 8 7 6 5 4 3 2 1

LSC-C

Printed in the United States of America

The new school year was just starting, and the morning train was crowded, as it always was.

Classes hadn't even begun yet, and I was already feeling down, when I noticed a girl in my grade nearby.

She held her phone right up to her face, careful not to bother anyone around her. This obstacle meant I couldn't see her face clearly, but her slender physique and smooth long hair were enough to tell me she was pretty.

Around her was a man who appeared college age, a businesswoman, and a salaryman. I recognized them from my everyday commute, except for the salaryman. Him I hadn't seen before.

False charges of sexual assault had been plastered all over the news and social media lately, so men—especially salarymen—tended to place their briefcases overhead, holding onto the straps with both hands...but this man didn't. He held the strap with one hand, and I couldn't see where the other was.

Then the girl suddenly stopped tapping at her phone.

It's April, the beginning of a new school term—new year, new life—and it kicks off with this?

Thinking something was amiss, I observed her more closely and noticed her phone was shaking more than it should. The train wasn't enough to account for it; I guessed her hand was the one doing the trembling.

Hey, college student, see anything out of place?

Okaaay… What about you, lady? …Nope. They won't take their eyes off their phones.

"Plea……it…"

The soft voice belonged to the girl.

Is it only me? Does no one else hear her?

Everyone around had earphones in. No way they'd catch that.

I hope I'm wrong, but if not…

"Excuse me. Excuse me. Sorry…"

I pushed my way through the densely packed train, earning me glares and disgusted frowns in the process, and forced myself between the two, facing the salaryman.

I was pretty sure the girl had said, "Please, stop it."

I wasn't brave enough to tell off a complete stranger, much less an adult man, but I couldn't bear to watch this girl shaking from how much she wanted him to leave her alone. I braced myself and glared at him a little.

The fortysomething man was wearing glasses; anyone would have pegged him as an upstanding citizen.

I scowled at him, and he adverted his gaze, faltering.

"The next station is…" I could hear the train announcement.

"Wh-what do you want? What are you looking at me fo—?"

"Could you please stop it?" I needed a ton of courage to say that, and I wasn't even the victim. I couldn't imagine how the girl must've felt when she was saying those same words a moment ago.

Despite the noise of the train along the tracks, it seemed like everyone around heard me.

"Huh? Wait, was that man groping him?"

Wait, me?!

"She's my friend. P-please stop bothering her," I said while pointing at my back as a sort of explanation for the onlookers. *We're from the same school, so that should be believable. Although I don't even know who she is.*

"Whoa, a molester? Gross…"

"Gropers are the worst."

The looks of disapproval made the man nervous.

"This dude was molesting a high school boy?"

I'm telling you it wasn't meee!

"A groper going after guys? Oh, that'll be juicy."

No, stop spreading rumors! Wait, what should I do now? Grab him and call the police? Would that be the thing to do here?

While I was thinking of my next move, the train arrived at the station, and the crowd flowed outside.

Wait, where's the guy?!

The culprit had taken advantage of the commotion and stepped outside.

"W-wait!"

I didn't have any obligation to pursue him, but I wanted to see this through to the end.

Thanks to the flock of people at the station, catching up to him was easy, and I grabbed his hand. That made a scene, which caught the station attendant's attention. I explained what had happened, and the man was taken into custody.

"Nice work, kid. And…what about the girl?"

Oh, she's not here. Guess she stayed on the train. Well, whatever. I doubt she would've wanted to be interrogated anyway.

By the time they had finished questioning me in her place, it was already past eight. My usual twenty-minute trip to school had taken four times longer than it was supposed to, and I was late on my first day.

I checked the class-placement announcement hanging at the entrance and put my sneakers into the shoe rack. Mine was the only empty slot, so finding it was easy.

The opening ceremony was already over, and all of the classrooms I passed by were already starting homeroom.

I found my new classroom, Class B, and stealthily crept through the back entrance.

The homeroom teacher was a woman: our English teacher from last year, Miss Wakatabe. She was wrapping up her introduction just when…

"Ryou Takamori. We already know you're late; there's no need to be sneaking around."

…she called me out.

"Oh… Okay."

Everyone turned toward me, some of them softly laughing.

The station attendant had offered to tell the school about my tardiness, and fortunately, everything had already been taken care of on that front. The teacher didn't scold me for arriving late while I found the one open seat.

Finally. I can catch my breath.

I decided to see who my next-door neighbor was, and it turned out to be Hina Fushimi.

"Again?" I murmured.

Fushimi was my childhood friend; we'd been together since preschool. Well, she wasn't exactly my *friend*, but I'd known her my whole life. And we'd always been in the same homeroom class.

We often ended up near each other at the start of the term, too. This was the fifth time we'd found ourselves in adjacent seats. I hadn't spoken to her since middle school, so we weren't really close anymore. Not to say we couldn't get along, though.

I looked at her while she kept staring straight forward at the teacher.

Her skin was pale white, her cheeks slightly flushed, and her lips were thin and moist with some kind of lipstick. Her long eyelashes brushed together with every blink; her legs were slender, wrapped in black knee socks, and the pleated skirt of her uniform wasn't too short or too long. Her hands were small, her fingers slim, her nails glossy.

It was as if Fushimi's whole body received a fresh coat of cuteness and prettiness every day. As someone who'd known her forever, I felt like I was watching a great piece of art slowly nearing completion.

Everything the teacher said went in one ear and out the other while I kept my mind occupied with such thoughts. Then Fushimi took out a pen and started writing something down in her notebook. She showed it to me.

Thank you for helping me out.

Helping her out?

The only "helping out" I could remember doing recently was speaking up back on the train. So...that was her? But how could she tell it was me? As far as I knew, she'd seen only my back.

Our eyes met.

"Oh... I heard your voice. And I took a photo."

She started tapping at her phone below the desk, then showed me the photo of what had been behind her then, taken like a selfie.

Yup, that's me and that guy.

"Were you all right?"

Fushimi gave a vague smile. Of course she wouldn't be all right after that. "He touched my uniform, but that's all."

That was a relief to hear. Seriously. If I hadn't noticed, or if I had decided to ignore it, things could've been worse.

"I'm glad you saved me," she said.

"And I'm glad you're okay."

"You were like a superhero back there, Ryou."

It was the first time since grade school she'd used my given name, which felt a little awkward.

"Let's forget about what happened today, okay?" I said.

She smiled bashfully and shook her head. "No way. I can't."

I didn't usually go around saving damsels in distress, so I thought it'd be better to put the whole incident behind us. Especially considering most people would rather forget about the horrible experience. So why had she replied that way?

I was still confused when Fushimi flashed me a smile that would out-shine a goddess. "Guess we're in the same class again. I'm looking forward to another year together."

"Oh, yeah," I replied shortly, still wondering why she was smiling like that.

I had no way of knowing then that a completely average dude like me would fall in love with Fushimi—an extremely beautiful, popular girl who just happened to be my childhood friend.

The next morning, I didn't see Fushimi on the train. Her house was close to mine, so she should've been taking the train from the same station as I did, but I never saw her on my way to or from school.

Come to think of it, I didn't know if that was because she took the bus instead, commuted by bike, or simply took a different train.

I got to school without anything notable happening and made my way to Class B's room, which was on the second floor with all the other second-year classrooms.

And there she was, already at her seat, surrounded by a cluster of other boys and girls. There was always someone visiting Fushimi during the breaks. Most of them were the popular kids who got all the attention, so it was awkward squeezing into my own seat right beside them.

"Good morning, Ryou," she called in that clear voice of hers.

The greeting interrupted their conversation, and everyone around her turned toward me. Their faces had *Who the hell is this?* written all over them. No surprises there. Introductions had already been over by the time I'd gotten to school the day before.

"...Morning."

Their glares hurt...especially the envy from the guys.

I took my seat and started tapping at my phone. Phones were a great way to avoid social interaction naturally. It helped me feel like I had a right to be here in the classroom.

While my antisocial measures were in full force, the conversation kept going—talking about club activities, the hot new TV series, and especially romance.

"Fushimi, aren't you going to join a club? You could join us in the girls' tennis club. We need more members."

"Sorry, I already decided not to do clubs in high school."

"Wanna make a group chat? Tell me your @, Fushimi."

They were all in on the fun, boys and girls. Quite a few of the dudes were going after her, I could tell.

It was spring the previous year when I realized that Hina Fushimi was a popular girl. And only because I saw an upperclassman asking her out. To be honest, it shouldn't have taken me that long.

I'd heard rumor after rumor, legends about the long list of guys who had asked her out or had given her their social-media handles or phone numbers.

Those rumors dated back to middle school, actually. In fact, I doubted they were just rumors, though back then I thought they were exaggerated.

Fushimi's appearance wasn't anything special to me since I'd gotten used to seeing her back in preschool.

The teacher arrived at the classroom, and the crowd surrounding Fushimi scattered to their respective seats. This happened every break, and I always prayed for the teacher to get there as soon as possible.

Very carefully, Fushimi scooted her desk over until it was right beside mine.

"Huh? What?"

Did she forget her textbook? …No, she's not usually forgetful.

The teacher started explaining whatever the day's lesson was while Fushimi spread her notebook between us on our combined desks.

Do you get what's going on? she wrote.

Oh, is she asking about the lesson?

"Yeah," I muttered, and she smiled.

Actually, I wasn't getting it at all—heck, I wasn't even listening to the explanation in the first place.

Math is hard.

Weren't you terrible at math?

Why do you *know that?*

I hadn't shown her my test scores once since we'd entered middle school.

W-wait, is that…a known fact in our neighborhood? Is my own stupidity what all the chatty housewives are talking about?!

I knew for a fact Fushimi got good grades, but not only because we were in the same class—my mom talked about it all the time. Maybe she got her intel from the same neighborhood network. Fushimi was arguably the prettiest girl in our school, and I was just some dude you put in the corner of the classroom. The simple thought of her caring about me made me nervous. I couldn't just slide in and say, *"Actually, yeah, mind giving me a lesson?"*

Then she showed me her notebook again. There was a drawing of some little…cat…thing, alongside a speech bubble that said, **Love!**

From what I could gather from our previous conversation, I guessed that meant that she loved math, so she would like to teach me.

"Yeah, makes sense. I mean, we're in the same class."

She was trying to erase the cat's speech bubble as I said that, and she stopped right in her tracks.

That seemed strange, so I turned and saw that her face was red as a tomato. Our eyes met, and she started stuttering and shuddering, then whacked her pencil case off the desk.

"Awwwawww…"

The heck does that mean?

She picked the case back up, then cleared her throat. She pulled herself together quickly, but her ears were still a bit red.

Was she always this jittery?

You didn't take the train today? I decided to write out what was on my mind.

"G-give me a second," she said softly, then started writing down her answer. *Usually my dad takes me to school since it's on his way to work. Yesterday, we had different schedules, so I took the train.*

Oh. Well, that explains it.

Man, what bad luck to run into a creep on the one day she had to take the train.

Thank you for saving me before it got worse.

"S-sure," I answered awkwardly, and she smiled.

Do you remember our promise?

Hmm? Our promise? What promise?

Fushimi looked at me with eyes full of hope while I tried to remember what that was.

Promise…? One thing was for certain: It wasn't one we'd made in middle school. But we'd made a whole bunch back in grade school.

Nope, no idea. I remember making promises, but I can't recall what any were about.

Around three minutes went by while I was thinking.

I glanced over and saw her cheeks were puffed all the way out, like a hamster about to explode. Busted—she knew I forgot.

Then she whipped her face away, like she never wanted to see me again in her life, and moved her desk back.

Huhhh? You were ready to teach me math but won't tell me what the promise was?

This wasn't the Fushimi I knew.

I mean, she was like that back in grade school, but then she grew up and became all calm and collected, never showing emotion on her face. At least as far as I knew.

Suddenly, a wave of nostalgia hit me. For a moment, the girl next to me wasn't the prettiest one at school, but little Hina, my childhood friend.

"I'll be the mom, so you be the dad, 'kay, Ryou?"

"Huh? Why? I wanna be the dog!"

Back when we were little, we played house this one time—like any kids would probably do. The expression on her face right now, sitting next to me in class, was the exact same one she'd had back when she was whining about being the dog.

She had her cheeks puffed to near detonation while she busied herself copying the text on the blackboard. Full hamster-bomb mode. The tension seemed to go all the way down to her hands—I could hear her mechanical pencil's lead breaking again and again.

What had flipped her hamster switch? Well…

Ryou, let's have lunch together!

Huh? Why? No thanks, I'm fine by myself.

…I said that. Or rather, I wrote it, during our notebook chat.

I had no idea why that hamster-fied her, but that was the apparent trigger.

After the last morning class ended, I took my lunch—a convenience-store meal—and left my seat.

I wondered if she would end up alone during the break, but no, she had a whole crowd around her, as she did every day. In fact, wasn't she better off without me?

I didn't really care about having or not having friends, but people who did care put a lot of importance on these first few days of the school year.

April was an exhausting time—you had to actively tag yourself as part of a certain group, let people know who your crew was.

Fushimi's eyes met mine for a second, and she had this abandoned-puppy look on her face.

Sorry. Your reputation is too much for me to have lunch with you now. I apologized in my mind and left the classroom.

I made my way to the physics room on the third floor of the special-classrooms building. It was always open, probably because there was nothing of value in there.

When I went inside, I saw someone had already arrived: Torigoe, a girl with shoulder-length hair who was a lunchtime regular in this room.

"You're here."

"Can't go anywhere else."

We exchanged unenthusiastic greetings, and I sat far away from her, like always. Then we started on our lunches, tapping at our phones without any real conversation.

Torigoe was the only person I got along with at school, although I only saw her in this physics room during lunch break. I didn't know which class she'd ended up in, and I doubted she knew mine.

We'd been like this since our first year—not really meddling in each other's business or talking about anything we didn't need to. We weren't really friends, more just two like minds.

"So what were you talking about with Her Highness during class?"

Despite the nosy question, she didn't seem particularly interested in the answer. She didn't even take her eyes off her phone.

"Oh, you mean Fushimi? Nothing, really."

"Uh-huh…," she replied absentmindedly.

"Wait, how do you know about that?"

"Because we're in the same class."

Seriously? I had no clue.

"It's also blowing up the group chat."

"...What?"

"Yeah, there's a group chat with, like, seventy percent of the class in it."

"The hell? And you're in it?"

"I mean, yeah. I don't talk, though. I just lurk."

Huh, that was unexpected. I didn't peg her as the type for a class group chat.

...And they didn't even invite me. Wh-whatever, not like I care.

"Well, I wouldn't join even if they asked."

And I did kind of wish they'd asked, at least. Even though it was true I wouldn't have joined. I'm a teenager, please understand.

Torigoe left out a soft laugh. "Oh, please, you don't have to pretend you don't care."

I'm not pretending!

Anyway, Torigoe told me how everyone was excitedly speculating about what I could've been talking about with Fushimi.

"Don't they have anything better to do?"

"From what I can tell, literally anything Fushimi does is the most fascinating topic in the school."

Seriously?

I doubted anyone knew Fushimi and I went all the way back to childhood. We certainly didn't act the part.

"It's just that nobody expected to see you two together. I was surprised, too. I mean, the perfect princess and the king of loners?"

"Wait, the king of what?"

It actually fit so well, it wasn't funny.

"Bw-wuh?!" Torigoe let out a bizarre screech. It was probably the first time I'd ever seen her lose her cool.

"What's up?"

"Huh? No, nothing... Huh... You don't know?"

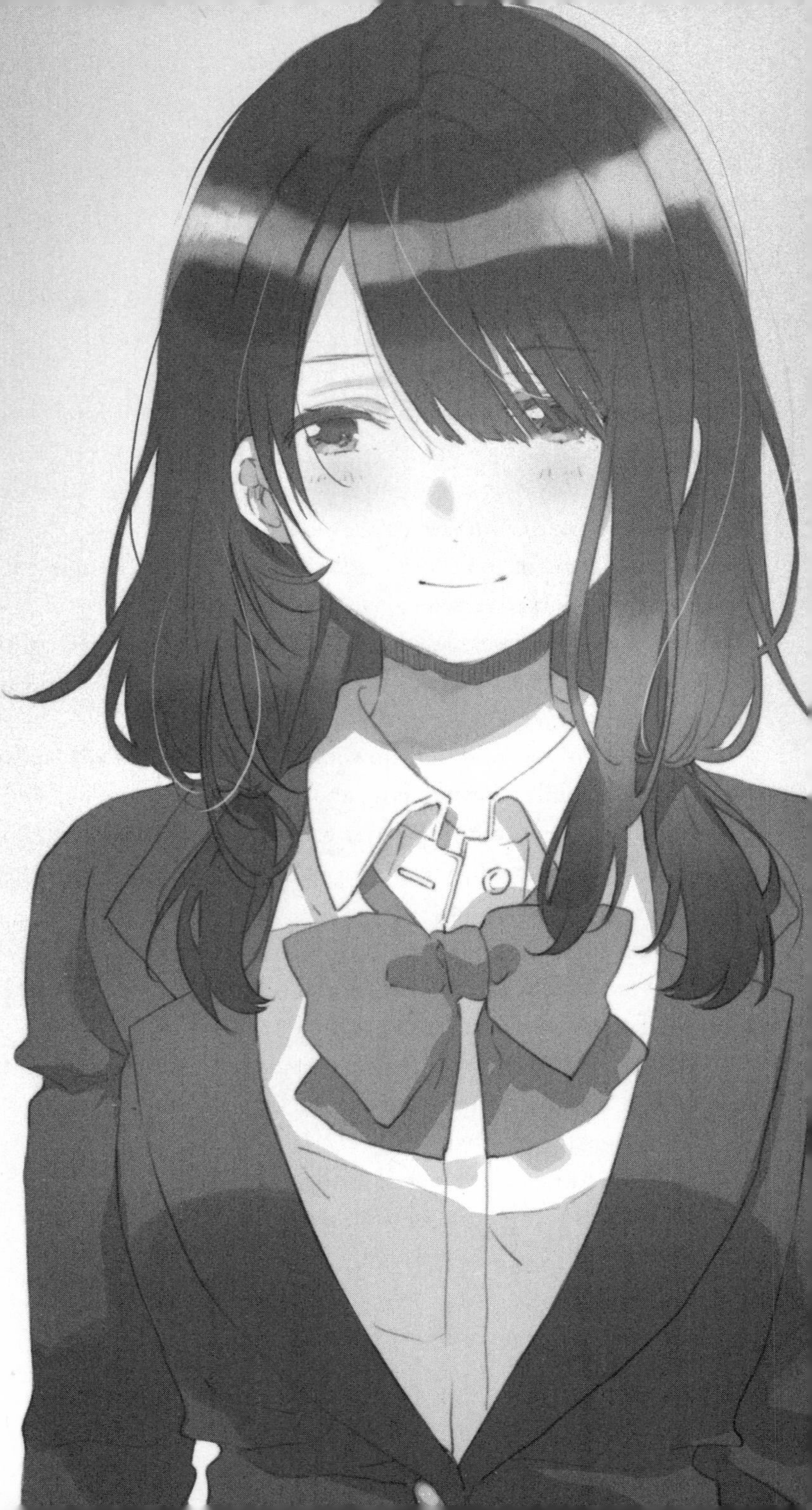

Who doesn't know what?

I was confused, but lunchtime had ended. We went back to the classroom separately.

As always, Miss Perfect Princess was surrounded by classmates. They had invaded my seat, too. *Sigh.*

I don't mind you using my seat, but lunch is over. Go away already.

It wasn't such a huge deal that I had to actually tell them off, but it was annoying.

Then Fushimi noticed me. "Ryo—er, Takamori is back. Would you mind leaving his seat?"

Nicely done, Fushimi!

A guy who was obviously dressed for attention reluctantly stood up. I gave Fushimi a thankful thumbs-up. Her calm and collected poise dissolved into a beaming smile.

These last few days, she had been different from my mental image of her. We had talked a bit the previous year, but she'd always kept that even expression.

Oh well.

Come to think of it, she started acting all cool like that back in middle school. I believe it was around the time when she started getting her reputation as the perfect and graceful pretty girl. She looked nothing like the person I'd known my whole life. And I honestly wasn't a fan.

I considered taking a nap when class started, but I felt the short vibration of my phone. Probably my sister asking me to go shopping for groceries on my way back home.

I checked my phone below the desk and saw an unfamiliar icon along with the username Hina.

...No way.

Next to me, Fushimi was sending occasional nervous glances at me.

I-it's her! But how did she get my profile? ...Was it Torigoe?

And why would she text me when we're right beside each other?!

Torigoe gave me your handle! Hope that's okay!

I mean, it's fine... Wait—there's more.

Do you want to go back home together today?

What's up with you, Fushimi? Don't you always go home with your popular friends? I've heard the neighbors talk about it. Plus, you sure it's okay? There's gotta be plenty of people who want to go with you.

I asked her all that with a glance, to which she shrugged, burying her head deeper and deeper into her shoulders.

She briskly tapped her phone and then looked at me again.

Is that a no?

I could feel that she was on edge. Why was she so antsy just from asking me that?

There was only one answer I could give.

sure

The "read" icon popped up instantly as Fushimi lifted her head from her phone and beamed. That smile made my heart skip a beat.

I was used to seeing her face, or I thought I was...but I was surprised by how cute she appeared to me right then.

4 Death (from Embarrassment)

Class was over for the day.

Were we really going back home together? I was skeptical up until it was actually happening, but, well…it was actually happening.

"Let's go, Ryou."

"S-sure…"

That stuttered syllable felt like the only word I could say to her anymore.

Fushimi grabbed her bag, stood up, and made her way to the exit. Her every movement was so bouncy I could almost see a musical note with every step.

"Hey, Hina," said one of her friends, "where should we go toda—?"

"Sorry, I'm going back home with Takamori today."

"What? O-okay…?" Fushimi's friend stared in shock.

As I walked after Fushimi, her friend studied me with some bemusement.

Yeah… Me too.

The girl had been in our class the previous year, and naturally, she never saw us acting all chummy. Really, no one would have thought we got along at all then. I had no idea why Fushimi was reverting to how we'd been in our childhood. You could also ask why we'd even stopped after grade school, though, and I'd still have no idea.

Fushimi rejected a couple more invitations from friends on her way out of the classroom. They were all similarly weirded out.

Yes, I get you. I don't understand any more than you. I still can't believe it.

I'd accepted the invitation only because I had no reason to turn her down, but still, how did this happen?

"You sure? You don't wanna go for some fast food or karaoke with them instead?"

"Huh?" She looked over her shoulder while combing her silky hair, uncovering her ear.

"I'm asking why you want to go home with me." Surely she'd have a way better time stopping by somewhere with them than going straight home with me.

Fushimi pouted. "I'm not telling you anything, you promise forgetter."

"What the...?" I pouted, too, and she laughed out loud.

Ah, dammit, this is kinda fun... Just like old times.

We exited the school building and walked side by side. Everyone was staring at us, even the first-years.

Now this is awkward...

"And I always go straight home after school. Just so you know."

"What?"

"In case you were assuming li'l Hina was the kind of girl to go out and enjoy the nightlife. I'm not."

Li'l Hina? What's with the cutesy act?

"And I don't think I like that being your impression of me," she was saying.

"Sorry, I assumed. You get along with the kind of people who seem like they do."

"Even when I do humor them, it's only for a bit. I always go home at, like, six."

So she's the model student in class and outside it, too.

Then what was the school princess, so beautiful she made the prettiest flower blush, doing at home so early?

We got to the nearest station in under five minutes and boarded the train.

"Oh," I accidentally said aloud, realizing why she had asked me to go home with her.

"Huh? What is it?"

"Fushimi, check out the train."

A question mark appeared above her head, but she took a look. Around half of the people inside were students, the other half were quite varied.

"What am I supposed to be seeing here?"

"The train isn't packed. No weirdos. It's all students like us."

"Yeah, and?"

"That means you don't have to worry about gropers on the way back."

"What? But I'm not?"

"..."

"I'm not."

"I heard you the first time."

"Then say something the first time. Wait... You think I was bringing you along for that?"

"O-o-of course not!"

"You're such a bad liar!" Fushimi flashed me an impish smile and poked at my chest.

Agh! Don't you tease me!

"Would you protect me again if the train was packed like that morning?" Fushimi seemed strangely peppy.

"Again...? I only did it that time by chance—plus, the train back home is never that crowded."

"Oh, come on! I'm speaking hypothetically! Don't be so nitpicky about the details."

Those "details" are kinda important, though.

She stared at me with a pout so I had no option but to sigh in defeat. "Y-yeah, I would. *Protect* sounds kinda embarrassing, but I wouldn't let anyone do that to you."

The bashful smile she gave me in return told me my answer was satisfactory.

"But I almost never take the train back home anyway," Fushimi said.

"There goes your entire argument…"

What even is this conversation?

It was true; I never saw Fushimi on my way home. I'd assumed that was because she didn't go home around the same time I did, but I guess I was wrong.

"Then why did you take it today?"

"Because…you…" She murmured something and stared out the window, flustered. I couldn't hear anything.

"Huh? What? I couldn't hear you, sorry."

The train swayed as Fushimi turned half of her face to me. Her voice was still quiet, but this time, I was able to get what she said.

"Because *you* take the train back home…!"

Her cheeks started turning red, and it wasn't only because of the sunset.

"And I'm the one…who wanted to go back with you…"

She looked down at her feet and fidgeted.

I still couldn't believe what she'd just said—or this whole situation, for that matter. This *had* to be a prank or something. Someone was around here filming and streaming it all.

"Huh? What? What do you mean?"

"Oh, come on! Please stop making me repeat myself! You're so mean! I'm gonna die from embarrassment!"

Don't even suggest it! Or I'll die, too!

After that, we didn't say anything until we arrived at our station.

Is this what going home with friends is supposed to be like?

I remember hanging out with people on the way home back when I was in grade school, but... what do high schoolers do?

"You're thinking hard. What about?"

Fushimi stared closely at my face. I squirmed.

"No, it's just... Was that it? Was that all you wanted to do?"

The walk from the nearest station to my house was only fifteen minutes, taking it slow. During my morning rush, I could make it in ten.

"So you're worried about that."

"Well, yeah. You're our school's princess, the brightest star."

"I don't want you to see me that way, too," muttered Fushimi, unamused.

I mean, how can I not?

"Oh, that reminds me, are you friends with Torigoe?" I asked.

"Torigoe? No, not really."

Torigoe giving her my handle had suggested otherwise, but it seemed I was wrong.

Come to think of it, Torigoe must have been surprised when she got that message from Fushimi.

"Hey, I want to make something very clear," declared Fushimi, stopping in her tracks.

"What is it?"

Make something clear?

I had no idea what it could be about.

"Are you—"

"Heyyy!" A very familiar voice interrupted her.

Fushimi pointed behind me. "Ryou, someone's waving at you over there. She's dressed like a *gyaru*."

Wait, is that...? Behind me was the oldest daughter of the Takamori family: my little sister Mana, now in her third year of middle school.

Her brown hair was slightly wavy, and her makeup was extremely loud and dramatic. The skirt of her school uniform was most likely shorter than allowed, and she had a cardigan wrapped around her waist. According to her, this would prevent her panties showing from behind, but it didn't stop the front from going public when she was on her bike.

Mana was waving her hand and skipping over to us.

"Who's that?"

"Mana."

"What?! Little Mana?! W-when did she start dressing so...so worldly?!"

Back when Fushimi and I still played together, Mana had joined us plenty of times, but any trace of that little girl was gone.

She was still more of the shy type when she started middle school. Who knows when she turned rebel and joined the *gyaru* fashion culture? Certainly not me.

My sister skipped all the way to us. "Bubby, you heading home?"

"Please don't call me that in public. Come on."

"But what else am I gonna call my bubby, Bubby?! Well, who's your friend? Oh! Hina! How's it going?"

"Nice to see you again, Mana."

Instead of starting a friendly conversation after so many years apart, Mana just stared at me, then at Fushimi, then back at me.

"That's weird. I, like, never see you with other people."

"It's coincidence. Pure coincidence."

"Uh-huh…" She snorted. "So anyway, Bubby, what do you want for dinner?"

"Stop calling me that, seriously… What about curry?"

"You got it." Mana let out a sneaky laugh.

Despite the stereotype associated with her style choices, she was more of the hardworking type underneath. She made dinner every day in place of my mom.

"Okay, see you later."

Mana got back on her bike and went off, probably to the supermarket to buy food. She only dressed like a party girl—she didn't play around outside.

"Wow, wasn't expecting that," muttered Fushimi. "She's real cute, but I wasn't expecting her to change that much."

I know, right? I agreed in my mind, as if this weren't my sister we were talking about.

"But I already know that you like that kind of girl. Right?"

"Wait, *what?*" I was so astonished it felt like my eyes would come out of their sockets. "Who told you that?"

"You. Back in middle school."

Middle school? Ah, you mean that one time?

There was one time when the other kids were teasing me pretty hard about me always being in the same class with a girl I'd known for years.

"You like her, right?" they'd say. *"I bet she wakes you up every morning!"* And so on.

So to stop them from making fun of me, I tried to think of the polar opposite of Fushimi's traditional charm.

"No way! I don't like girls like her. I'd rather date a gyaru.*"*

Fushimi had a more conservative sense of style, so I went for the least conservative type there was. I was basically talking out of my ass, though. I can handle being teased, but not when it comes to girls.

Fushimi started walking sluggishly. "And you were so enthusiastic…"

What a good memory!

"I didn't mean it! It was just a spur-of-the-moment thing, nothing serious."

"Mana grew up so much and changed, and…and I…"

She might follow some wild city trends, but the only thing that grew up about her is her chest.

Fushimi looked down at her chest, which had only a gentle change in elevation on a mostly flat surface.

"…Now I want to die…"

"Don't give up on living!"

Her shoulders slumped as she continued walking.

"I'm serious. I'm not into *gyarus* at all."

"Really?"

"Yeah. I just said that because they were teasing me about our friendship. I didn't mean it."

I was sure many of them were perfectly nice, but I honestly preferred keeping them at arm's length.

My sister was an exception—both *gyaru* and good girl. She did cook for me, after all.

"If you say so…"

She felt somewhat relieved…probably.

"Geez, so there was no reason for that distance at all."

Thinking about it, I realized the first year of middle school might have been when I started feeling that emotional distance—my childhood friend Hina becoming my classmate Fushimi.

It was partly my fault, since I wanted to stay away from her to stop the teasing. It was all because I started seeing her as a woman, but that's part of being a teenager. Everyone goes through that stuff. Like measles or something.

"Wait, so…you started giving me the cold shoulder because of what I said then?"

"That's right. How could I not feel bad about it? Jerk."

That whole thing was a grudge?!

"I'm sorry. Seriously." I begged for forgiveness several times. "Wanna go somewhere? My treat, as an apology... How does that sound? Just make it, like, ice cream or a snack. I can't afford café pancakes or anything like that."

"In that case...," she replied, "I want...to visit your house."

"Huh?"

Fushimi said she wanted to visit my house.

Naturally, my house wasn't a café, and we didn't serve pancakes. As for ice cream…we did have some in the freezer. I also happened to have some snacks I hadn't opened yet, so no problem there. Mana would get mad if we ate them, but this was an emergency.

I couldn't tell what Fushimi was really after here, but I answered ambivalently. "Yeah, okay."

My house happened to be on the way to Fushimi's, so a pit stop was easy, with no backtracking. But…why?

I turned to look at the prettiest girl in school, who was walking beside me. She was smiling, and the expression wasn't quite the same as the Hina Fushimi on display in the classroom.

I told her multiple times there wasn't anything interesting in my house, but she replied that it was fine. She was in her little-Hina mode from our childhood, which meant I had no idea what she was thinking.

Before I could figure any of it out, we reached my home.

"It's been so long since I came here!"

It was the same Western-style house from back then.

The parking spot for the pimp ride—that was what I called Mana's bike—was still empty.

My mom should be at work, so I guess no one's home.

…Is it okay to let a girl in when no one's home?

Fushimi blinked her long eyelashes a few times and tilted her head sideways like a little bird.

"What's the matter?"

Her face wasn't the only reason for her 100 percent approval rating among the boys—it was these mannerisms, too. I immediately understood how her fans felt.

"No, it's nothing…"

She had visited many times before, and plenty of those times, we'd played in my room. Still… I started feeling queasy.

I opened the door, let her in, and gave her some slippers. She thanked me while taking off her shoes and slipping her small feet in.

Now, where do I take her? We've played in the living room before, so…

"We're not going upstairs?"

"Bwuh?! My room?! Y-you sure?"

"Yes. Let's go!" Fushimi already knew the place, so she went right upstairs, her slippers echoing against the floor with every step.

I've got everything she shouldn't see out of sight, right? Thank God my mom taught me to always put away my things after using them.

"C'mon, you come up here, too."

Fushimi was already at the top of the staircase, her head turned to look back at me.

"I'm co—"

It was the perfect angle—I could…I could… Nope, I couldn't see up her skirt.

"…"

"?"

I was relieved and slightly disappointed at the same time.

Is the length of that skirt calculated precisely for this? Nah, there's no way.

Hiding my disillusionment, I went up the stairs and past her. I walked through the hallway and opened the door to my room.

There were some clothes and manga lying around but nothing pornographic. Once again, I felt relieved.

My room was about a hundred square feet and had a simple interior: just my bed, a desk, and two shelves for manga.

"Wow, it's all cluttered," she muttered, peering into my room from behind me. "But it's just like I remember it."

I stepped inside and picked up my clothes from the floor to put them on the bed.

I think I had some cushions in my closet.

I looked for something to sit on, and Fushimi just up and sat on my bed. I instinctively glared at her.

"Oh, sorry. I can't sit on the bed?"

"No, I don't really mind it, but…"

What do you think would happen if I didn't have morals? I'd have you pinned there, ready to get down to business!

"Hmm? But what?"

"Fushimi, you should be more cautious. You're too suggesti—" I broke off when she lay down on the bed.

"Suggestive? You mean like this?"

"Okay, come on…"

"Ah-ha-ha." Fushimi rolled around laughing while I sighed.

"When was the last time you came to my house? Middle school?"

"No, it was in sixth grade, on…" Fushimi paused at a strange spot in her reply, still staring at my ceiling.

Sixth grade? Really?

"In sixth grade, on…what?"

She turned her back to me. "You don't remember, Ryou? That day in sixth grade was the last time."

I have no idea. That day? What day? Didn't you hear me say I thought it was in middle school? I can't remember.

©Fly

"So do you want tea or juice?"

"Gosh, you're so bad at changing the subject." Fushimi laughed out loud, still lying down. "Juice, please."

After she told me, I left the room and headed for the kitchen.

"Sixth grade? Yeah, we played together like five days a week back then... Agh, it's so hard remembering specific things with her... We spent so much time with each other, it all blends together..." While I was muttering to myself, I poured two glasses of apple juice. I took a bag of chips and went back to my room.

Since I didn't have a table, I put them on my study desk.

"So what happened when we were in sixth grade?"

I turned around and saw her still lying on my bed. *Sheesh.* I sighed.

My glance glided from her shapely nose to her well-defined eyebrows. Her large, pretty eyes were closed, and her lustrous hair spread all around her on my bed. I could hear her faint breath escaping through her thin peachy lips.

"A-are you asleep?"

She cracked open her eyes and looked at me.

Is she just pretending to be asleep? Is this supposed to be a continuation of that suggestiveness talk we had?

"Fushimi, please stop messing with me already. And don't forget not all guys are like me."

I'll teach her a lesson.

I straddled her body, putting my hands beside her face.

What now? Are you scared?

O-oh God, this is closer than I expected... Now I'm the one getting anxious.

Fushimi opened her eyes wide. Her expression was unexpectedly serious.

"I'm not messing with you. It's just that you forgot."

"C'mon, tell me what it was."

"It was one of our promises."

That's the thing... I can't remember them all.

Now, one single promise would've left a bigger impression.

"You do know doing this—lying around in a guy's bed and pretending to be asleep—is something you should only do with the one you love, right?"

"...You're stupid." Fushimi blushed and looked away. "Stupid."

"Why'd you say it two times, stupid?"

"You're the stupid one! You forgot our promise!"

Agh, there's no winning this!

"How long're you gonna stay there anyway? Get off me."

"Ah, sorry."

I instinctively rolled off.

The mood got kinda awkward, but we started talking again once I broke out the snacks. She even started folding my scattered clothes, saying she needed to do something with her hands while talking.

After a while, Fushimi grabbed her bag and stood up. "It's time for me to go," she said.

It was already getting dark outside. I offered to take her home, so we walked under the streetlights carving a path in the darkness.

"I'll concede on me being stupid, but please just give me another hint."

"A hint? After all those promises we made...I'm in shock, honestly." Fushimi pouted.

"I'm telling you, I'm sorry."

"No, it's fine. Sorry for being mean. Of course you forgot something from that long ago. Although, I have all our promises written down."

"For real?"

Now that she mentioned it, I did remember her taking lots of notes.

"You even said you'd do it, too, you know?"

"For real?"

"For really realsies."

Actually, I do feel like I have something written somewhere.

"Hey then, couldn't you just show me what you wrote? I'll do my best figuring out which one it was."

"You...will...?" Fushimi got so red she started steaming. "N-n-no! I mean...th-there's a lot there beside just our promises. It's too embarrassing."

"Hmm... I see."

So she wants to keep that dark past buried.

We eventually reached Fushimi's house.

"Thanks for everything today. See you tomorrow."

"No problem. See you."

Fushimi waved her hand, and so did I before turning my back.

I wonder if I can find my memo pad.

Once I got back home, Mana and my mom were already there.

Mana was preparing dinner, while my mom was smoking right below the ventilation fan.

"Welcome back."

"Ah...yeah. Hi."

"Hey, Bubby! We're having curry tonight! It's almost done, so sit tight!"

"Yeah, cool," I said while lying down on the sofa.

My mom was always busy with her nursing job, so Mana took up all the house chores. Mom took on more of a fatherly role—it was uncommon for her to do things like cook or peel me from bed in the morning.

"Hey, Mama, did you know Bubby came back home with Hina today?"

"Oh, did he?" Mom started grinning, the cigarette still in her mouth.

What are you, some mischievous middle schooler?

"Hey, don't go telling her that!" I snapped.

Mana turned around and stuck her tongue out.

I gotta change the subject.

"Do we still have my notebooks from back in grade school, by any chance?"

If I remembered correctly, they should be in storage here somewhere.

Fushimi said she had a special memo pad for our promises, but I didn't remember getting one myself. If I did take notes, they'd be in my school notebooks.

"Ah, yeah, we have some of them in the closet."

Mom put out her cigarette and headed to the Japanese-style room. I followed her, and she opened the sliding door. She stuck her head in and started hunting for my books.

"They should be around…here." She took out a cardboard box that had my name written on it. "So what are you looking for?"

"Well…it's…nothing." I evaded the question and started looking inside.

"Oh, c'mon, you can tell me, my little Ryou." She put her arms around my neck and started poking at my cheek.

"Stop it."

She just laughed.

Why does she always act like one of those friends who's a "bad influence"?

My mom had me when she was still young, right after she started working, and that led to her marriage. She was still in her forties, when most moms of kids my age were older. My dad passed away in an accident when my sister and I were still little, so my mom took on the father role, too.

"Are you going out with Hina? That's why you went home together, right?"

"Of course not."

"Really? When I saw Mana so upset about it, my woman's intuition told me something was going on. I was like, 'This definitely isn't just walking home together!'"

"Well, don't believe everything your 'intuition' says. Nothing's going on."

You can only think that because you don't know how popular she is with every other guy in the class.

I didn't have any special talent; nobody in class cared about me. Why would she like *me*?

"You're not? But you were so close back then! I remember clearly how she came to tell me 'I'm going to marry Ryou!' all the time."

"Wait, she did?"

"She's still adorable, of course, but Hina back then was an absolute angel."

I don't remember any of that.

I continued searching the box until I found my notebook of miscellany from fifth grade. Most of its contents were terrible drawings and random scribbles—no promise memo was to be found.

"...Huh?" Something had been ripped out.

What's with this? I wondered, when the smell of curry reached my nose.

"Mana turned out to be a good kid, despite the *gyaru* thing. How about you marry her instead?"

"We're siblings."

"Ha-ha-ha. You're right."

"Mama? Come help!" The shouting came from the kitchen.

"Coming, coming," Mom replied, standing up and leaving.

"The promise memo...the promise memo..."

I took a look at other notebooks until I found it in my sixth-grade math notebook.

I'll have my first kiss with Hina when we get into high school.

Wait, whaaaaaaaaaat?!

Wh-wh-what the hell?!

The note stood out among the formulas and rows of numbers.

"What was I thinking?!" I rolled on the floor.

I-it's even more embarrassing seeing it in writing!

But I guess...this is what she meant?!

Fushimi said the last time she came to my house was when we were in sixth grade. The note was dated February 15. The day after Valentine's.

Did we promise this...? Did we make this mortifying promise then?

Fushimi had cut herself short earlier. She'd said, "*In sixth grade, on...,*" then blushed. Maybe she'd meant to say, "*on Valentine's Day*"?

Yeah, now I get why she didn't tell me.

But why high school and not middle school? I can't imagine it being me who set those terms.

Meaning it had to have been Fushimi's idea, and I'd accepted without thinking it through.

My first kiss... You little... You stupid little kid! Had I watched a drama on TV or something?

In that case, what had happened back when I returned to my room after pouring the drinks now made some sense. If I were less principled, I would think she was inviting me and had taken the chance, so she was waiting for that to happen...

"G-giving a sleeping girl a kiss?! I'm not doing that, stupid!" I threw the notebook back in the box.

"Bubby, what's with all the fuss? What's that about a kiss?" Mana was standing there, arms crossed, dressed in her uniform plus an apron.

"K-kiss...? I-I was thinking out loud! 'Man, Mana's tempura is... chef's kiss.'"

"But you said you wanted curry. Why tempura now?" Mana gave me an icy stare.

"...I know."

"Also, you ate my chips, didn't you? Your plate better be totally clean after dinner."

"I'm sorry... It will be."

"And...there were two cups in the sink. Why?"

Th-there's no escaping her wrath. G-gyarus are so scaryyy!

"..."

Wait, why am I in trouble here?! Because I ate her chips without asking? Because she thinks I won't finish my dinner because of that? Or because...I let someone in...?

She was still glaring at me. "So many annoying things happened today."

Ah, all three. A reverse royal flush of crappy luck?

"Mana, just so you know, I didn't do any—"

"Go kiss your tempura by yourself." She tried to kick me, but I stopped the blow.

I'm not about to get beaten up by my little sister!

"Eek! H-hey, lemme go!"

"You're gonna kick me if I do! Maybe if you didn't shorten your skirt so much—!"

"I do what I want!"

And there are the panties… This is why gyarus *have such a bad reputation!*

Mom realized something was amiss, because Mana wasn't coming back, so she returned and scolded us both.

I ate my dinner quietly, like a cat spending a week with another family.

"The curry's really good," I said.

"…Well, duh."

Mana seemed just a little bit happy.

My phone's alarm woke me up, and I ate Mana's *gyaru* breakfast. That was what I called her little set of toast, eggs sunny-side up, and salad.

By the way, Mom had just gotten back from her night shift, so she was still sleeping.

"Bubby, you're running late." Mana hurried me while putting on her heavy *gyaru* makeup.

You're so lucky, being in middle school. Your school is so close by.

I gulped down the toast with milk, and my little sister yelled again with genuine worry in her voice. "No, seriously, you'll be late!"

"Yeah, yeah," I replied while grabbing my bag, then went outside.

"Good morning, Ryou."

There was Fushimi, flashing a smile as warm as the spring sun.

"G-g-good morning. Why are you here? Ah, did you leave something at my house?"

She tilted her head to the side and laughed softly. "No, that's not it. Wanna go to school together?"

"Huh? Oh… Okay."

But why? I had many questions but no time, and we hurried to the station.

I guess her dad couldn't take her today, either? And she's traumatized by the groping attempt, so she can't take the train on her own?

"Hey, Fushimi, in case you didn't know, some of the cars are women-only. You don't have to worry about gropers there."

"Hee-hee. I know, dummy."

Then why…?

"I'm not trying to bring you along as my bodyguard. And I wasn't yesterday, either, by the way."

Then why? What do you get from going to school and back with me?

Fushimi continued, "Plus, you can't get on the women-only car, right?"

"Well, yeah. I'm not a woman."

"Then I won't get on it, either. I wouldn't get to go to school *together*."

I didn't quite get it, so I gave a vague reply. "Um… Okay…"

Fushimi bumped me with her shoulder for being so dense. "Is it wrong to just want to go to school together?" she asked bashfully.

Hey, it's too early in the morning to get my heart pounding with that expression.

I tried as hard as I could not to show anything I was thinking on my face. "I—I guess it's fine."

"Good. Hee-hee. You look happy."

How can you tell? Dammit, this is pathetic. It's even worse when she realizes I'm trying to hide it.

Fushimi seemed eager to live out the childhood-friend clichés.

We went through the ticket gate, then entered the train heading to our school. It was packed again—not full to bursting, but there wasn't enough space to really move around.

"Mugh…," groaned Fushimi from inside the crowd, unsure how even to pass through the masses.

She was about to be squashed in between the businesswomen and salarymen, so I reached out to grab her and pull her to my relatively more spacious side.

"Th-thanks… I thought I'd be crushed alive…"

"You're welcome."

I took the weight of the crowd behind me, putting both hands on the door to keep some of the pressure off Fushimi.

"Is this the legendary wall pin of love?"

"Yeah, yeah. What else can I do? Hope you don't mind."

"No, it's just a joke. Thanks."

Her face is so close. Unable to look straight at her, I averted my gaze. *And she smells so good. Is that her shampoo?* I tried to rid my head of worldly thoughts, praying like a monk. *Just two more stations…just two more stations…*

As another form of distraction, I tried looking outside the window, but as soon as I turned my head, the train swayed greatly. Our heads smacked together.

A-ah, did my lips…touch her? They did, didn't they…?

It was so instantaneous I didn't really feel it, but I was sure I—

"_____!"

Fushimi was red as a tomato, her mouth curved in an upside-down V shape.

Why is she blinking so fast?! What's going on? Is she trembling?

So they really did! I was supposed to make sure no one harassed her, and now here I am!

I started blushing, too, as I began to understand the situation.

"I-I'm sorry! It wasn't on purpose, I swea—!"

"R-Ryou…don't kiss me like that…"

"I didn't! I did not! So, um, where was it?"

"R-right here." She pointed at her cheekbone, just below her eye. "G-geez… You made me blush…," she said with such saccharine sweetness that I could taste the sugar, then she put her head on my chest.

"I'm sorry," I apologized, patting her head a few times.

"I-it's fine… I forgive you…," she replied softly. She was red to her ears, her head still on my chest.

The announcement for the next station played, and the train stopped.

Other students wearing our school's uniform started leaving. Some of them gave us strange looks, though they couldn't see that this was Hina Fushimi.

There was no one left waiting for people to step out, so I told her, "C'mon, we've gotta go."

Still unwilling to pull away, she shook her small head and sent her silky hair swaying back and forth.

"Huh? ...But we'll be late."

Then she nodded. Even as I urged her to get off, Fushimi grabbed my sleeve tight.

"...I want to stay here, with you."

The announcement played, and the doors shut with a thud.

Skipping classes wasn't anything new to me, so I didn't really feel opposed to her idea of staying on the train.

The train had been full of students from our school, but now we were the only two. Seats were now open, so we took two beside each other.

"O-oh no… Now I'm corrupting you…"

"Oh, c'mon, it's not that big a deal."

Fushimi was almost tearing up, but I smiled at her.

I had no idea where we were going or when we were getting off, and I doubted I'd get a clear answer if I asked.

As far as I could remember, Fushimi had never arrived late at school or skipped classes.

"Seriously, don't worry about it. I do this all the time."

"Yeah, I know."

The train went on to another station and another— We were getting farther and farther away from school.

"I wasn't planning for this. Sorry," she said, apologizing multiple times. Every time, I reassured her it was no problem.

"I doubt anyone cares about me," I said, "but everyone's gonna lose it once they know you're late and didn't even call ahead."

"Uh… Yeah, probably." Then she murmured, "Maybe I'll say I had a stomachache."

Can't you come up with a more creative lie?

I searched for the school's number, which I had saved in my phone, and told it to her.

"Why do you have the school's phone number?"

"So I can lie about being sick and skip classes whenever I want."

"Wow... Ryou, since when are you such a delinquent...?"

"Oh, please."

We got off the train at the second-to-last station so we could call the school.

Fushimi tried to make the call while we were still on the station platform.

"Hey, hey! They're going to hear the announcements if you call from here." I recommended that she do it in a restroom.

"Oh, you're right! You're not a veteran truant for nothing, huh?"

"Who do you take me for?"

Fushimi came back from the restroom after five minutes. "A...clerk?... answered the phone and said she'd relay the message to Miss Wakatabe."

Apparently, she hadn't asked Fushimi anything. The deed was done without trouble.

"She just said, 'Okey dokey.'"

"Wow, I would've been thoroughly interrogated... That's how it went in first year, in fact..."

"I guess they just really trust me."

"And not me. Dammit..."

"Ah-ha-ha," she laughed. "Now that we're here, want to stroll around?"

With that, we exited the station and decided to wander around town.

There were few buildings around the station, most likely because the terminal was right near the foot of the mountain. The only cars nearby were the couple of taxis parked at the roundabout.

We enjoyed our hike, walking wherever Fushimi's whims took us.

I was worried some police officer would ask us what was going on, but nothing happened. There were hardly any people, let alone cops.

"Ah, I can smell the sea." The thick scent of the shore clung to my nose.

"Huh? The sea? Is it close to here?"

"Maybe."

We kept walking until we reached the national highway, which had much denser traffic, and saw a windbreak at the other side. We glimpsed the white sand and blue ocean peeking through the trees.

"It's—it's the ocean!!"

"Lower your voice!"

Fushimi was as excited as a dog in the snow. "L-l-look! Ryou!"

"Calm down, geez."

"S-sorry, it's just that it's been such a long time!" Delighted and giddy, Fushimi ran off toward it.

"Hey, wait!" I pursued her.

We found a crosswalk on the highway and went past the windbreak to the beach.

"Wowww!"

Even though it wasn't her first time there, Fushimi was lost in the moment, her eyes gleaming. She held her hair to protect it from the wind and walked through the crisp sand to the shore.

We'd come together to this same beach before, back during summer break in sixth grade. Back then, Fushimi had drawn an umbrella in the sand and told me to write my name under it, on one side on the handle. Then, blushing, she'd written her own name on the other side.

Ryou ♡ Hina

What an embarrassing pair we were back then.

It was nine AM. All our classmates must've been in class by then.

"Wh-whoa!"

At a sudden gust of wind, Fushimi held down her skirt as she stood in front of me.

I took off my uniform's blazer and gave it to her.

"Here, wrap this around your waist. I don't want to be flashed, either."

"But all the sand will stick to it."

"Doesn't matter."

"...Okay. Thanks."

She tied the sleeves together at her waist, just like Mana always did with her cardigan, and picked up a stick. She started writing in the sand.

I love...

Slowly, she turned back to me.

"Oh, yeah, I figured."

"Huh?!" Startled, she buried her head between her shoulders, then smiled bashfully. "S-so you really noticed...?"

"Anyone would. You're so excited about it."

"Huh?" Fushimi's expression turned serious.

"You love the sea. That's it, right?"

"...Huh?" A cloud crossed her face.

"You're not talking about the se—?"

"No!" She puffed her cheeks. Immediately after, they turned red in embarrassment.

She changed from one emotion to the other so quickly; I'd never seen her like this at school.

"...Gosh... Stupid."

She was staring at me through her lashes, but the look was both angry and embarrassed.

So you meant me?

But I couldn't ask that. What if it was another wrong guess? What if she wanted me to give her advice about someone else or something? The possibilities were endless.

And if you did... Why?

After all, Fushimi was the most popular girl at school. I was just her childhood friend. That would be the only reason to choose me. There had to be lots of other, way better guys. I bet some of them had already asked her out.

"Tell me, who do you think I'm talking about?" she asked with mischief in her eyes.

"Let me guess. It's a handsome actor who happens to be named Ryou."

My answer was so wildly incorrect that Fushimi's face went blank, and her eyes took on a dull sheen.

"Yeah. That's it."

There was no emotion in her voice.

Look, if this were a manga or an anime, I'd get it. The childhood friend going *Ryou, I love you!* is so typical. But the characters' relationship in those cases is unbreakable. They're together their whole lives.

As for us, I hadn't really spoken to her since way back in middle school.

She never came to wake me up; we didn't go to and from school with each other. Our families didn't go on outings together.

I sat down on the stone steps to try to calm down. Fushimi quickly followed my lead and sat down beside me. She wrapped her arms around her legs, making her dainty body even more compact, then buried her face in between her knees as if it might make her invisible.

"Ryou, you really do like trendier girls."

"I already told you, that's not true."

How many times do I have to repeat myself?

"You might not be aware, but I'm actually quite popular."

"Yes, I know."

Well, at least she can tell. I mean, how could she not?

"You think nothing when someone else asks me out?"

"No, I do." I did have my own thoughts about it—many of them, in fact.

Fushimi raised her eyebrows, surprised. "Really?"

"Really. I couldn't picture you going out with someone. Considering how many guys you've turned down, I just assumed you'd keep doing it."

"That's all?"

"Once I got used to it, yeah. Before that..."

I stared into space, thinking back on things.

I didn't know when exactly I started getting used to it, but I thought it might've been around our first or second year of middle school.

"Before that, it did get under my skin. I was sure they only asked you out because of shallow reasons, like they only thought you were a pretty face or whatever."

In retrospect, that was more than enough reason for a middle schooler to fall in love with a girl.

"Yeah, they were shallow, all right," Fushimi said. "I mean, how can you say you like someone you've never even talked to before? Most times, I could barely put a name to their face, and I told them that when I said no. Figured it was kinda like fans with a celebrity."

I totally get you.

I mean, if someone you'd never spoken to before showed you affection and demanded a yes or a no, you'd go with the latter.

"Yeah, the general impression the guys had was that you always said no, so they'd try it out just for fun without expecting anything."

The potential risk involved in asking Fushimi out was quite low because the probability of her saying yes was also low.

"Yeah... Now that's shallow. And shameless! If they were serious about it, I might consider thinking it through myself, but getting asked out 'for fun'? Why would I ever say yes to someone I don't really know and who doesn't even care?"

The more I heard her talk, the more sense it made why she'd never dated anyone. Surely not everyone was like that, but they were the majority.

"You said you were annoyed, right? Why?" she asked.

"Good question."

"You weren't…jealous, were you?!"

"No wa—"

No…way? Really?

"'Nooo! Another man will take my dear Hina from meee! What an annoying jerrrrk!'…kinda stuff?"

"I don't talk like that."

But it's true I was annoyed…

Was I afraid that I would lose an old friend once she got a boyfriend? Or could it be a more…*romantic* emotion…?

No, no, no, no, no.

"Hee-hee. You're really thinking this through."

"Well, I don't know if my feelings were romantic or not…but yes, I was probably jealous."

That was an embarrassing thing to say to her face. But it was true.

Fushimi was staring at me. "…Can I scooch closer?"

Even after all these years seeing her face, it was as cute as ever. I felt like I was going to pass out and die, but I tried to keep my cool.

"Sure. Fine."

"Okay, then…" She came closer, pushing her shoulder against mine. "Hee-hee-hee." Her face melted into a smile.

"You're enjoying this too much."

"Well, you're smiling, too."

I am?

I rubbed my face with both hands.

"…Guess I'm turning into a delinquent, too."

"What do you mean?"

"…I don't want to go back to school. I want to stay here with you."

"Hey, you don't have to be good all the time."

"Yeah. Then let's be bad. Just for today."

We decided to skip school entirely.

©Fly

After a long while staring at the ocean, we headed to a convenience store for lunch. Then we wandered about aimlessly. There were no fast-food restaurants of any kind—only homes and small shops lined the streets.

Void of cars or even people, the quiet atmosphere was perfect for conversation.

"So I don't remember most of our promises, but there is one I found."

"Really? What is it?" Fushimi's eyes shone with joy.

"That we'd have our first kiss when we entered high school."

"Auh!" She froze in place. "Y-you sure remembered a big one..."

"I didn't remember it; I found my notepad. After I read that, everything you did in my room made way more sense."

"That's...embarrassing..."

I smiled awkwardly.

Restless, she asked quietly, "B-by the way, y-y-you wouldn't h-happen to have had your f-first kiss already, w-would you?"

She babbled and stammered her way through.

Why's she beating around the bush? Oh, actually, she starts talking like that when she has a hard time saying or asking something.

"Not yet." The reply was uncomfortable for me, too. "O-of course not. You should be able to tell just by watching me at school."

"No, I can't. I have to make sure. I-i-if I don't, then you could've broken our promise! I had to! You can never be sure!" Fushimi was flailing her hands around.

Oh right, she's never said yes to anyone asking her out. Or maybe…that's because she already has a boyfriend…? Everything would make sense in that case.

Maybe she was in a secret relationship, like a celebrity escaping the eyes of the press.

"Anyway, I'm glad…because…I haven't…either…"

I had to do a double take when I heard that. "No way."

"Yes way! Why would I lie about it?"

My gaze instinctively went to her lips—thin and soft, slightly damp.

"Is that so surprising?"

"…"

Her lips have never…

"…Hey?"

If she's intending to keep her promise…I'll be…the first?

"Are you listening?"

"Uhhh?! Huh? What was it?"

Crap, I stared at her lips for too long.

I shook my head to get rid of my earthly desires.

"It's just…there's a lot of rumors going around about me, and I wondered if you believed them, too."

"Ah, that's what you're worried about?"

I guess even popular people have their own problems. Wish I could have that problem for once.

"I don't believe them, but you are, like, perfect at school. On the surface, I mean. You're good at both academics and sports, and you always get along with everyone. But that's also why I can't see who you really are beneath that layer. It's hard to know what you're thinking. It feels like you're hiding something, so I do get where they're coming from."

"I am aware of my reputation as the beautiful, perfect girl."

"I bet you'd have an easier time of it if you acted this way around other people, too, instead of just me."

Although a lecture from a guy with no friends probably isn't that convincing.

Fushimi kept her gaze down and quietly said, "But that's…because you're special…"

God, now that's a killer line.

"What's the matter?"

And she doesn't even realize.

I had to change the subject.

"You started getting more attention with the way you dressed after summer break in our first year of middle school, remember? You also started putting on makeup and all that."

Her skirt also got dangerously short.

"Ahhh, that takes me back. So you do remember, huh?"

All it took to make my friend happy was remembering something about her.

"I can't forget how bizarre it was to me. You did look great, but it felt like you were forcing yourself. I couldn't believe how much you'd changed after one summer break."

"I didn't undergo a complete transformation or anything. I realized it didn't fit me and stopped right away."

It probably felt even stranger to me because I didn't actually like *gyarus*.

"My mom was worried about you back then. She thought you'd made some bad friends."

"I—I know… The entire neighborhood was talking about it…"

Just so you know, though, everyone in our neighborhood had great respect for my sister.

She greeted them every day *even as a gyaru.*

She properly parked her bike *even as a gyaru.*

She was charming and friendly *even as a gyaru.*

Does she get a free pass because she's pretty or what?!

I did the exact same things, and I'd never been complimented on it.

"I think Mana's following in your footsteps, though."

"What...?"

She knew about the free-pass system?!

Fushimi tilted her head to the side. "Is it me, or did you take that the wrong way?"

As our conversation continued, we found ourselves all the way back at the station, which I recognized from our trip here.

"It's still barely past noon?"

"Yeah...," Fushimi replied.

We started talking about what to do next, when I felt my phone vibrating in my pocket. It was a text from my mom.

You skipped school, didn't you?

How do you know? You're not even at home.

I had a missed call from school. They say no one called in about your absence.

Crap... Right... I forgot to call the school myself.

So? What's going on?

She usually filled her texts to the brim with emoji—the complete lack of them told me she was 100 percent serious.

Fushimi wondered about my sudden sweating outburst and took a peek at my phone.

"Oh man, you're gonna get it when you go home."

"The worst part is that Mom will tell the *gyaru* with a heart of gold not to make me any food."

"Rest in peace."

Hey, don't kill me just yet.

"Should we go to school?"

"Y-yeah. As long as we get there, it'll just be a tardy."

Although we still skipped classes.

"Sorry. It's my fault for forgetting to call in."

"It's fine. I just realized we'd still be together anyway since we sit next to each other." She giggled bashfully. "Hee-hee."

you're screwed, bubby

I was typing my excuse to fend off any questions, when I got a short text from Mana, followed by a ton of demon and *X* emoji.

Ugh… I'm not getting out of this one. They're gonna take away my food!

Fushimi and I arrived "fashionably late" just in time for the second afternoon class: English. Being that our homeroom teacher was in charge of that one, she called us out on it.

She didn't question Fushimi too much, but she had me pegged as a continuous offender.

"Takamori, you're late? When did you get here?"

"Um, just now…"

"Well, it's no skin off my nose whether you call in or not. You're the one getting in trouble," she replied sardonically, then started class with a broad smile.

I knew what she meant; I could feel it in my soul. I was in trouble.

Fushimi scooted her desk right beside mine. She flashed her princessly smile. "I forgot my textbook… Can I see yours?"

"Sure."

But I had seen it.

I saw you take your English textbook out, act like you just had an idea, and put it away again.

"Good thing you brought yours, huh?" She was lying with a straight face. Zero shame.

…You were right. You are turning into a delinquent.

I put my textbook in between both of us, then decided to take whatever notes I needed while I was writing my apology letter for Mana.

"What's wrong?"

"I might actually starve, so…" After hitting send, I received a reply in a matter of seconds.

im not the one you should be apologizing to

Right. Nothing for it but to beg forgiveness from Mom.

I was thinking about what to tell her when…

"Takamori, can you tell me what word goes here?" the teacher asked.

Agh, she's looking at me?!

"Um, well…"

Crap, I wasn't paying any attention! …And that's why she chose me, isn't it?!

The teacher smiled devilishly. She was reveling in my suffering, making an example of me for the rest of her students. *This is what happens to naughty kids who don't pay attention.*

I stared at the blackboard, then at my textbook, but I had no idea.

Then Fushimi tapped her desk and scribbled something down in my blank notebook.

what

I glanced at her, and she nodded.

"*What*, ma'am."

It seemed my answer was right. The teacher shot me a dull glare, like she'd found some broken toy. She was not amused.

"…Yes. In this English sentence, you…"

Class resumed, and I gave a sigh of relief.

Thanks

You're welcome. Fushimi was grinning ear to ear. Be more careful from now on, okay?

OK

Waka's got the eyes of a hawk.

Waka was the nickname for our teacher, Miss Wakatabe.

Yeah, I can see.

She was also calling out everyone else not paying attention—people dozing off, people chatting with their neighbors, people daydreaming. This had been the case since the year before. You could never lower your guard during her class.

After the lesson, we were handed review tests.

Eh, these don't really matter. I'll just fill it out with whatever.

Then Fushimi leaned toward my desk.

A pleasant aroma tickled my nose every time she moved, being so close.

"Let's see, this one is…"

"C-c'mon—it's fine."

"Huh? But…this should be easy. Just look at the textbook."

Wait, really?

"Look—it's here. As you can see in this sentence…"

Fushimi thoroughly explained how to answer.

We're taking the same class… How can she get this stuff so much better than me?

And we had been taking all the same classes even before now, so when exactly did I go wrong?

"There. You should be able to solve it now."

"You're really smart, huh, Fushimi?"

"Hee-hee. I know, right? Please go on. Praise me more," she said with a bashful smile.

"Listen up, everyone. After this, we have homeroom, where we'll appoint our committee members, okay? We're the only class that hasn't done it yet, so I'm not letting any of you go home until it's done!" The teacher gave the last announcement before leaving at the end of the class.

We'd taken some time for that the day before, but we hadn't reached an agreement.

Aside from the class reps, we had to choose members for cleaning, library, health, and all sorts of other committees. Half the class had to participate somewhere.

That last part was the problem—no one wanted to do any of it. We'd drawn lots the year before.

"Ryou, are you joining a committee?"

"I don't want to, if I can avoid it."

"Figures," she replied.

The prettiest girl at school moved her desk back to its place and was instantly surrounded by a crowd of other girls. They chatted about the committees, why she arrived late, and lots of other stuff.

Oh, the trials of being popular.

When the bell rang again, the teacher came back and started writing down each committee's name on the blackboard.

We had to choose one boy and one girl for each.

The teacher sat down on her folding chair, with the backrest in front of her.

"So how did you choose last year? Drawing lots? See, I believe lots aren't dramatic enough…"

Dramatic? What? What are you talking about?

Probably everyone else thought the same.

"Agreed. Dramatism…is important."

Except for my childhood friend.

I'm pretty sure everyone wants to just be done with it and leave already, though.

"Let's start with class representatives. Anyone can apply for themselves or nominate someone else!"

Ryou, want to join one together?

What if Fushimi nominated me for class rep?

After further consideration, I didn't particularly mind. I wasn't so opposed to joining a committee that I'd turn down someone else's nomination.

"…Okay, then." I slightly raised my hand, to which the teacher reacted with obvious shock.

"O-ohhh! Now that's a surprise! The prince of truants! Who would've thought?!"

The prince of truants? Well…you're not wrong.

"Not like I have much motivation, but if you don't mind…"

"Accepted! Everyone, give him a round of applause," the teacher said cheerfully while kick-starting the clapping. Some of my classmates followed.

"Ryou, I didn't expect you to go for class rep."

"Someone's gotta do it, and I figured it might as well be me."

Fushimi blinked in amazement, then nodded with determination.

"Okay, now for a girl. Who will be the other class rep?"

The classroom had been in complete silence until then. The balance was now broken, and unrest spread among everyone.

"Takamori as the class rep… What an unexpected twist. Now this is what I call dramatic!" Our thirtysomething teacher nodded in satisfaction.

"Me!"

"Me."

Just as Fushimi raised her hand, someone else spoke up.

"Wow… Fushimi and Torigoe…"

Huh? Torigoe?

"Torigoe?" Fushimi turned around to face the seat behind her, and so did I.

My lunchmate had her hand raised, her face calm.

Fushimi and Torigoe's simultaneous volunteering provoked a strange wave of commotion in the classroom.

"""""Oooohhhh!"""""

"The quiet beauty versus the princess..."

"M-my bet is on Torigoe! The diamond in the rough."

The guys started muttering a bunch of stupid stuff to one another.

Meanwhile, my childhood friend kept her hand raised up high, stoic as a swordswoman facing her opponent.

Yeah...she's not giving it up.

"Whatever shall we do? Talk it out? Rock-paper-scissors? Draw lots? No, that would be too boring." The drama lover stirred the pot.

What will they do? I wondered, watching the two of them as a totally innocent bystander.

"...I concede." Torigoe lowered her hand.

Fushimi snorted. Her face had *victory* written all over it.

"Ah... You do? Well then, our class reps will be Takamori and Fushimi," the teacher declared, and everyone turned to stare at us.

By then, Fushimi had replaced her smugness with her usual graceful smile.

She changed that much in a second. Astounding skill.

We stood at the front of the class to lead the remaining committee appointments.

"Looks like I have nothing left to do here now that Fushimi is taking over," Waka said with relief.

What about me? Why not mention me?

"Okay then, I leave you in charge." She left.

The mood lightened up now that the teacher was gone, and a few scattered conversations broke out.

"Next up, the cleaning committee. Anyone want to join?" Fushimi presided while I assisted. Probably for the best if we wanted things to go smoothly.

And Fushimi's influence did seem to grease the wheels of the operation.

"How about you, Yuuto?" said one girl. "Wanna join?"

"Oh, fine. Guess I will."

The committee was formed by a known couple.

"Ugh." "Ugh!" "Ugh." "Ughhh!" "Ugh."

I heard multiple groans all around the classroom at the lovers' flirting.

Serves you right. Get a room; no one can stand couples that are all over each other like that.

"We're in public, here… You shouldn't be joining the same committee together just because you like each other…" I shook my head. My comment was low enough that no one would hear it, but Fushimi was right next to me.

Wait, why do you suddenly seem inconsolable?!

"Y-you're right… That's not a good reason to…"

Oh no, no, no, no, no.

Her eyes were welling up with tears.

"What's wrong, Fushimi?! Everyone's looking at you—calm down!" I whispered to her.

She looked around, and her tears quickly dried.

That was fast! What are you, an actress?!

By the way, the "diamond in the rough," Torigoe, joined the library committee.

Yup. Perfect fit.

I stared at her face. I didn't have a real impression of it, since we never really looked at each other while talking or having lunch together.

I could recognize her when I saw her, but if someone had told me to picture her in my mind, I would've had a hard time remembering.

Then a guy stood up with a thud, holding a sports bag.

"Where are you going, Yoshinaga?" Fushimi immediately called to him.

It hasn't even been a week since we started classes, and you already know everyone's face and name?

"We're done here, so I can go to my club, right?"

"What? But class hasn't ended yet…"

This homeroom was the last class for the day. The main objective was appointing committee members, and the teacher wasn't there anymore. There should be no problem with leaving class early—only ten minutes were left anyway. In my opinion.

However, Fushimi didn't seem to share that opinion.

"Are we doing anything else?"

"No, not really…"

She was still as diligent, fastidious, and unyielding as ever.

"Then I'm leaving," Yoshinaga said, a bit annoyed. Fushimi kept quiet.

Waka did leave her in charge. And she trusts her a lot.

She had to keep the teacher's trust and fulfill her responsibility as class rep, but she didn't know how to argue her case.

"Stay at your seat for just another ten minutes, please." I bowed my head, and the classroom went silent.

Huh? Did I say anything weird?

I heard the chair being pulled again.

"…Fine. Sorry for getting so grumpy."

The bag dropped loudly to the ground, and Yoshinaga sat down.

"Thank you."

Everyone else let out a sigh of relief, then shot curious glances at me. I could imagine what they were thinking: *Whoa, who would've thought he'd say something like that?*

I knew it wasn't quite like me to butt in, but I had to help Fushimi out.

"Thanks, Ryou."

"Oh, no problem."

"Hey, hey!" Kurano called to us. She was friends with Fushimi and had also been in our class the previous year. "You two seem to get along really well. What's up with that?"

The guys' scowls were turning murderous.

No one had brought this up since the school year started. The blood-thirsty dudes weren't the only ones interested—the girls seemed quite curious, too.

"Ah, yeah. We've been friends since we were kids."

Apparently, not many people knew about this. I could tell, especially with the boys: Their lust for my blood calmed down visibly.

"Oh, so that's why."

"Childhood friends…"

"This is like, classic high school drama!"

"Anyway, yeah…"

""""That means they're never getting together!"""""

Fushimi chuckled. With a mischievous look on her face, she asked me, "Do you think so, Ryou?"

"Wh-why do you ask me?"

"Why, I wonder?" She beamed.

"Takamori and Fushimi are childhood friends!"

The news spread even further once classes ended, which made people think us going back home together was a normal occurrence.

All the dudes used to give me the side-eye before, but now that they knew about our friendship, they concluded that I presented absolutely no risk.

The silent comments changed from *Screw that guy* to *Oh, the childhood friend* and *Our princess is in safe hands*.

Then, in some sort of bizarre strategy to use me to get to her, a lot of guys showed up asking to be friends with me. All this during our short trip from the classroom to the school entrance.

"The school princess's power is really something."

It's like I'm her retainer or something.

"Huh? What was that?" Fushimi tilted her head to the side.

"Nothing." I shook mine.

We were walking home now, already far from school.

"Hey, Ryou—thank you for your help with Yoshinaga."

"It was nothing, really. No need to thank me twice."

"I wanted to say it again. You saved me."

Please, it wasn't that big a deal.

"On one hand, I don't blame him. Sports clubs have the spring tournaments coming up soon. On the other hand, you're as uptight as ever, huh?"

"What? No, no, no. Not at all. This is normal."

I wonder.

"Wh-what's that look for?"

"Remember when you, Mana, and I shared a shortcake, way back?"

"We did?"

"You were bawling your eyes out because you couldn't slice it into three perfectly even parts."

"...I—I was?"

In a way, I was Hina Fushimi's walking Dark Past–opedia. I had a huge list of her failures and embarrassing moments in my mind.

"You sure did. You were all like, 'Nooo, we can't split the strawberryyy!' Mana and I were super weirded out."

"I—I don't remember any of that! You're making stuff up!"

She refused to look at me while insisting again and again it wasn't true.

It was obvious she did remember, though I wasn't sure whether I'd had to jog her memory first.

"I'm not trying to make fun of you. I was just thinking about how you like to follow the rules."

"I can tell you're insulting me... Just look at that huge grin on your face..."

Fushimi glared at me and blushed, either because of embarrassment or anger.

"First of all...why do you remember that stupid incident and forget our important promises?!"

The counterattack hurt; I'd teased her too much. I didn't have a response.

"How many of those promises are there?"

"You don't even know that? Geez... There's as many as there are worldly desires in Buddhism."

"Are you kidding me?"

That's, like, over a hundred, right? No way I can remember that many...

My last gleam of hope was my promise notes, but I wrote them in random grade-school notebooks. Maybe I could find one that I'd saved for that purpose, but I had no clue.

We took the train and arrived at our station. After crossing the ticket gate, Fushimi whirled around, making her skirt swish in the air.

"Let's say good-bye right here for today."

"Oh, okay. You going anywhere?"

"Hmm? Ah, well, um, yeah, something like that!"

What a vague answer. Her expression was also strangely stiff.

"Where are you going?" I asked.

"Wh-why do you care?!"

Now I'm suspicious... Oh well—I shouldn't be prying if she doesn't want me to know.

I ignored her weird behavior, and we parted ways.

When I got home, Mana was in the kitchen.

"Nuh-uh, I'm not helping you out this time. Nope. No way." She wasn't usually this harsh.

"Please, Mana. Sis. Don't do this to me."

She stopped chopping away with the knife, then turned her head toward me.

Once before, I'd asked her if cooking with those gaudy nails was hard, to which she'd replied, *"Only an amateur would ask that question."* Okay. Sorry for being an amateur. What would a pro ask, then?

"It's so out of the question there's not even a question. Mom was very clear about it. What were you even doing skipping class?"

"...Huh? Well, I...missed my stop..."

"Then why didn't you go back? If you'd taken the next train in the other direction, you wouldn't have even been late."

Ugh. She's too damn smart.

I couldn't tell her Fushimi had asked me to stay on the train.

"What're you grinning about?"

"I-I'm not!"

©Fly

I really couldn't take any more of this. I knew it was my own fault, but having to skip dinner was too much.

"Then how about a snack?"

"The chips you stole were all I had. I haven't bought more."

No way out.

Guess I'll curl up and suck it up for the night...

I considered getting something at the convenience store, but my wallet was empty.

Right then, my phone chirped with a text.

I'll be there in a minute.

It was Fushimi. The time was already past seven PM.

sure, but why?

My text was marked as read, but she didn't answer back.

After a short while, the doorbell rang. I opened the door before Mana could get there.

"What is it?"

"Um...this!" She actually said "Ta-daa!" out loud while taking out a box wrapped in a handkerchief. "I made you dinner."

I was pretty sure I saw a halo shining bright behind her already dazzling smile.

"Thank you. Really."

"You said they wouldn't let you have dinner, so..."

She was still in her uniform.

So she went to the supermarket, then got cooking right away? For me...?

I was stunned.

"Oh, don't get so emotional... I wanted to make it. For you." She flashed a bashful smile, the kind she never would at school.

"W-wanna come in?"

"No, it's so sudden, and it's already late. I wouldn't want to barge in like that." She smiled like an angel, then said, "See you tomorrow," waved her hand, and left.

"She made dinner for me…" I immediately went back to my room to eat it.

I opened the box with excitement, and what greeted me was the color brown. It was chock-full of boiled pumpkin.

"Th-this is…a dinner? …Not her leftovers?"

She'd wrapped it up like a typical box lunch, so I was expecting, you know, an actual meal.

I mean, I like boiled pumpkin, but…I'm not sure about this!

"Eat up!"

She probably thinks her surprise dinner was a big success. I mean, it certainly was surprising!

"I remembered you saying you like these."

Yeah, but you gotta balance it out!

My boxed dinner was more like boxed pumpkin.

"Oh well, I do like pumpkin… And I am hungry."

Despite my complaints, I ate the whole thing. It was good.

"Bubby, Hina's here."

I woke up to the sound of someone calling me.

It was seven o'clock, a full thirty minutes of missed sleep before my alarm rang.

I begrudgingly sat up from my bed to make sure I hadn't been imagining the voice, and I got my answer when I saw Mana in her apron, standing in the doorway to my room.

"Why exactly is Hina here?"

"How would I know?"

I looked at my phone and noticed I had missed calls from Fushimi since six thirty.

...*Is it an emergency?*

"I figured you must be starving, so I made you extra breakfast today."

"Thanks... You'd make a great wife, y'know?"

Gyaru-ness notwithstanding.

"Wh-what the hell are you talking about?! It's too early in the morning for this!"

I reckoned I shouldn't go out in my sweats, so I put on a coat before heading to the entrance.

"Good morning, Ryou."

"Morning."

"I came here to wake you up, but I guess you were already awake. Good, good," she said while patting my still half-asleep head.

"Isn't it too early for that?"

"You think so? I always wake up at six thirty."

And that *is too early. It's a whole hour before I wake up!*

The way from home to school was only around thirty minutes, including both the train and walking. Homeroom started at eight thirty, so leaving home just before eight o'clock gave me more than enough time.

"Now that we're class reps, we shouldn't be arriving late. The thought had me up and at 'em this morning."

Her eyes were clear and open. Meanwhile, mine were still groggy and struggling not to close.

Fushimi was already transformed into her usual honor-student self. "Mind if I wait outside for you?" she said.

"Sure, if you want to."

"Thanks," she said before walking out.

Now I couldn't go back to bed, so I headed to the dining room to get my fill of Mana's breakfast.

"So why's she here?"

"Um...to pick me up?"

"Was Hina always the type to do that?"

It was the sort of thing a childhood friend would do, but it wasn't her style. Although, she had done it a couple of times when we were in the early years of elementary school. *Actually, those are kinda fond memories.*

"Are you two going out?"

"Bwuh?!" The miso soup gushed out of my mouth. "No. Not at all."

"Uh-huhhh," she answered back after glancing at the entrance.

I quickly finished breakfast and got ready before going outside and finding Fushimi, who was waiting for me and killing time on her phone. We headed schoolward right away.

Based on my observations of the previous year's class reps, the job didn't have much to it.

They said the greetings and farewells at the start and end of class, collected everyone's homework and gave it to the teachers, relayed the teachers' announcements, and did other similar chores.

We also had to coordinate the class during events, but I knew I didn't have to worry about that with the diligent princess and her powerful sway over everyone on my side.

The school day came and went, and when it was over, I was writing in the class journal when I noticed the girl sitting beside me was staring at me.

"...What?"

"Oh, nothing. I was just amazed at how much effort you're putting into this." Fushimi smiled at me.

I can't do it with you staring at me like that.

I wrote down a summary of the day's classes, then closed the journal.

That was when I became aware only the two of us were left in the classroom.

I guessed Fushimi got bored of staring at me: She was now face down on her desk, relaxing like a cat at home.

Now we just had to take the journal to our homeroom teacher, and our class-rep duties for the day would be done.

"So what do you talk about with Torigoe during lunch?"

"Nothing, really."

"Seriously?"

"Yup. We only glance at each other like *Oh, so you came*, then eat in silence."

It had always been like that. The lack of conversation never made it awkward for us or anything.

"I wonder why she volunteered, too," she said.

"Huh?"

Fushimi puffed her cheeks, and I stared very closely at her, as if she had the answer written there.

"To put it on her transcript or something?" I mused.

"Ah... Yeah, we'll be third-years next year."

It was a blind guess, but apparently, that was convincing enough for her.

We walked through the quiet hallways, bags and journal in our hands. Occasionally, we'd hear the muffled practice of the brass band in the distance.

"Did you also do it for your transcript?"

"Anyone who truly cared about that would never skip class like me."

"Yeah, that makes sense."

If anything, it was the mood in the classroom then. Everyone was expecting someone else to do it. I didn't like that feeling.

I worried someone with a big mouth—in many ways—would take over the class, and that would come back to bite me.

We left the class journal at our homeroom teacher's seat in the staff room, then made our way to the entrance.

The clouds beyond the windows were turning dark, and just when I thought it might rain, waterdrops started hitting the windows and drawing lines on the glass.

The rain was already so strong you could see it coming down by the time I changed into my sneakers at the entrance.

"Ryou, did you bring an umbrella?"

"No. The forecast didn't say there would be rain."

"Hee-hee. I suspected this might happen, so I—"

"Oh, a spare umbrella!"

There was a black one in the umbrella stand. It wasn't someone else's—everyone understood it was there for the community, in case of emergency. Part of the unspoken rule was to return it after.

"Oh? Y-you found one?"

"Thanks, whoever put this here. Oh, were you about to say something?"

"N-no! I wasn't!" She shook her head and both hands hard.

"Really?" I asked again, opening the umbrella up. It was too small for the two of us, but it was better than nothing.

We walked through the downpour straight to the station.

"I might get wet if we don't get closer… Is that okay?"

"How about I do this?" I held the umbrella so it leaned more toward her. *She shouldn't get wet now.*

"Then *you'll* get wet," she complained.

"Only my shoulder. It's no big deal."

"Oh, c'mon." She inched closer, her shoulder touching mine. "Now we're good."

Well, I'm not. This is too close.

Thinking back, I remembered that Fushimi drew an umbrella on the blackboard way back when.

"Ryou, let's put our names under the umbrella!"

"Why? What's that?"

"They say if you do this, you'll marry each other!"

"I've never heard of it, but I don't think that's how it works."

Maybe she still believes that legend or whatever she was wrong about.

…Huh? What is that strap sticking out of her bag?

"And then…later, I said…" She was talking quite enthusiastically, but I was more intrigued by the mysterious object.

I leaned closer and noticed the strap was coming out of a handle.

…Is that a folding umbrella?

"Fushimi, did you bring an umbrella?"

"…Huh? N-no…why would I?" she retorted, turning away.

Hey. Look me right in the eye.

Fushimi panicked and pushed the strap and handle down into her bag.

"…"

"…So as I was saying…"

"Don't change the subject!"

Fushimi gave up and pouted. "I-is that so bad? What's the harm? I've just…always wanted to try…sharing an umbrella with the one I love." She furrowed her brow sulkily. "…I just wanted to try it in real life," she muttered embarrassingly, her cheeks red.

I couldn't help but smile. I never saw her blush like that at school.

"Are you laughing at me? Geez!" she snapped, but then smiled.

The rain seemed to be just passing by—it had already stopped by the time we arrived at the station. Fushimi's shoulder was touching mine the whole way.

On our way home, Fushimi asked me about her "boxed dinner," since I hadn't touched the subject myself.

"Oh, the food you brought me?"

"Y-yes. Did you eat it?"

"I did. It was good."

Fushimi's grin was like a ray of sunlight against the cloudy sky. "I see, I see. So you liked it. My childhood efforts are finally being rewarded. I've always been good at making boiled pumpkin."

...Just that? What's with the weirdly specific skill?

Come to think of it, I'd always liked sweet food. Candies and stuff, of course, but also regular entrées on the sweeter side.

"Now I can strike one off the list."

"List? What's that?"

Her smile was gone, her eyes now as cloudy as the sky. "Here we go again...the Forgot-All-My-Promises-with-My-Childhood-Friend Syndrome. And yet you remember the weird parts."

...Syndrome?

"Did we promise you'd feed me a metric ton of boiled pumpkin?"

She looked away, fully annoyed now.

"In that case, I want to tell you something, too. Please add some sides and rice. You can't call that a boxed dinner, lunch, or any kind of meal. That's just leftovers. It's like you made too much and then handed it out to your neighbor."

After that comment, her cheeks reminded me of a puffer fish.

"You're awfully proud of yourself right now, aren't you? Stop it."

That strangely hurt. Low blow.

"That wasn't my intention" was all I could manage to reply back.

I won't be able to say anything again if she starts countering like this!

Fushimi stayed quiet, until she looked at her toes and muttered, "I mean… I can't make anything else… I just wanted you to say it was good…"

Crap. I lose this round.

She didn't look as if she was saying it just to win the argument. She really felt that way.

If she was actually trying to manipulate me, she'd act the exact same way she did with our classmates. She cared about me—and I couldn't say I minded.

After all, she did say it was on her list. That meant we'd actually promised each other this, and I'd probably said I wanted to eat as much boiled pumpkin as I could, or something stupid like that.

"Thank you for making my favorite dish."

"Yes…"

"If you ever want to do it again, it's okay if you try making something else."

"I'll just tell you now, I'm not as good as Mana."

"It's fine. No one is ever good at the start. And I'll eat it all, so don't worry."

Her face melted into a smile. "Okay, then… I'll do my best."

Now I wouldn't have to go through the shock of pseudo leftovers if there ever was a next time.

We continued to the Fushimi home so I could see her off, when she suddenly remembered, "So where's the box?"

Ah. I left it in my room.

"Sorry. I'll clean it and give it back tomorrow."

"No, don't worry—I'll take care of the cleaning."

"No, I..."

"It's fine, it's fine."

I felt bad about making her clean it on top of having her make me dinner, but she was insisting so stubbornly that I had to give in.

"I-in exchange...mind if I go to your house again?"

D-don't say that with a blush on your face! Now I'm blushing, too...

We won't do anything. Nothing. Nothing will happen. I'm not the kind of guy who'd take advantage of our friendship. Not in a million years.

Okay. Everything's good for me now. Act natural. Nothing happened.

"S-sure...if you wanna."

"Are you nervous?"

"N-not at all."

"Really?" She tilted her head.

When I let her inside, my sister's loafers were there at the entrance. She was already home, and it seemed she had heard us arrive, because the pattering sound of her slippers was approaching.

"Bubby, were you fine with that rain out...there...?"

"Hello, Mana. I'm hanging out here for a bit today."

"O-okay. Welcome..." Mana was bewildered. She blinked again and again, staring at me, then at Fushimi, then back at me. "Bubby... What are you planning on doing...bringing her home?"

"Nothing special. What are you asking? She said she wanted to come."

Mana turned to look at her, asking with her eyes whether that was true or not.

"Y-yeah. I did."

"Um... Okay, gimme a second. So she only acts pure, but underneath it all, she's after all the boys. God...my mental image of her is crumbling to pieces..."

"N-no, I'm not! That is *not* what's going on here!" Fushimi objected, her face red.

"Bubby's a virgin, Hina, so watch out. They're always on the lookout for a chance."

"Stop right there, Sister. I'm not that thirsty."

Also, how the hell do you know I'm a virgin?

"You should thank me for being here. My presence will work as a deterrent."

"I'm telling you, I'm not doing anything."

I thought I could see steam, which I immediately found out was coming off Fushimi's red head while she was staring at the floor.

"...I-I j-j-j-just remembered I have s-something to do. See you!" Fushimi's voice cracked as she ran away.

"This is your fault for teasing her."

"I'm not teasing anybody. I'm just stating the facts. Besides..." Mana looked away, her face quite red herself. "I—I don't want to...be hearing all the thumping and creaking from the second floor."

"Ah yes, pretending to be pro wrestlers. Nothing else."

"I don't mind if you do it when I'm not here. But um...d-do you have...you know what?"

No, I don't know what.

Given that I showed no reaction, Mana said, "I mean this..." Embarrassed, she made a circle with her fingers.

"...Money? ...No, I don't have much, really."

Determination flared up in Mana's eyes. I could almost see her thoughts: *I have to pick up the slack for my bubby!*

"Leave it to me. It'll be a bit embarrassing...but I'll go get them at the drugstore."

Get what?

That night, we had a Japanese-style dinner: boiled *hijiki* with grilled fish, meat-and-potato stew, and miso soup.

Mana really would make a great wife, even if she doesn't exactly look the part.

Mom was back from work, so the three of us had dinner together.

"...Mana, did you get a boyfriend?"

"Huhhh? No. Why?"

"Really? Then why did you buy...um...rubbers?"

"Whaaat?!" Mana froze up.

Rubber? Like a rubber band for her hair? She does tie it up quite often.

"D-did you see me...?"

"No, not me. Our neighbor Mrs. Tanoue saw you at the drugstore."

"B-but I was so careful!"

"She said you shouldn't be playing around with any man who'd ask you to get those."

"Haaah?!"

Man, sure is a lot of shouting tonight.

At least the miso soup is good.

"Ugh, this is so humiliating... This is your fault for being a virgin."

"What are you talking about?"

How do I have anything to do with any of this?

"I'm saying you should do your research!"

I had no idea what the fuss was about, so I could only take my little sister's scolding in silence.

"So that happened last night," I explained to Fushimi on our way to school the next morning.

"Oh... Poor little Mana..."

"Huh? Why?"

"Sometimes, I sometimes can't tell whether you're too sharp or too dense, Ryou."

I'm the bad guy here? I can't take much more of this. No one even tells me what the problem is.

We kept walking while I was still frustrated, and someone else greeted Fushimi, "Good morning!"

It was a girl in our grade, though I didn't know her name. She had her hair up in a short ponytail and was carrying a sports bag, so I figured she was someone from one of the sports clubs.

"Good morning," the princess replied with utmost elegance. Her smile was so royal I could imagine her giving a loftier greeting, like *"How do you fare this fine morn?"* or something.

"So you're going clubless, Hina?"

"Yeah. I already decided I wouldn't join any more for high school."

The girl's friendly smile instantly faded away, her eyes now cold.

"Oh. Okay. Sure, I guess playing around is more fun."

"That's not what I meant..." I could see the confusion in Fushimi's smile.

"If you ever change your mind, you'll be welcome in the track-and-field club. You get along with everyone already, so."

"Yes. Thank you for inviting me."

The girl shot me a quick glance before leaving to join a group of girls with similar bags.

Fushimi was good at sports; she was in the track-and-field club in middle school and did great at sprints and long jumps. From what I'd seen of her during PE, she was no slouch at ball sports, either. I'd seen a lot of people from small sports clubs asking her to join.

"They're still asking you even in second year, huh?"

"Yeah…" She seemed tense.

"I think you should just tell them you don't want to if that's how you feel. That'd be best for everyone."

"Girls also get offended by that sometimes, Ryou."

…Girls sure are a lot of work.

But Fushimi was right. She'd already gotten a cynical remark so obvious even I noticed, just now after politely declining. That girl had basically said, "*Wow, it's so great you have no responsibilities, huh?*"

"Who would ever want to join a club with someone who says those things?"

"I just annoyed her a bit."

Fushimi's really kind. There's no need to cover for her, y'know?

"If I joined any club, all the others would be up in arms, asking why I didn't join *theirs* after they tried to scout me."

The more I heard her talk about it, the more disgusted I was by the community of our school.

Fushimi's expression stayed grim, as if she was still worried about what the girl had told her. Anyone would be down after being mocked like that so early in the morning.

I rubbed her back a few times.

"I don't think it'll help to tell you to not worry, but… Well, let's just focus on what we have to do right now."

Not that that sounds very convincing from the delinquent who never listens to the classes he does *attend.*

"Thanks. Yeah, you're right. I'll do what I have to do." Fushimi's small hand formed a fist. Her expression brightened back up again.

I would've been too worried to do anything if those clouds had been gathering next to me all day. With some relief, I took my hand off her back and put it into my pocket.

"…Keep doing that."

"Wha—?"

"The rub-rub…please."

Rub-rub? Ah, you mean rubbing your back?

But why are you so red?

"It…calms me down. The touch."

I was about to reply, "*Sure, it's no problem*," but then I noticed how many students were all around us. We were close to school already.

"No, we shouldn't do this now…"

"Okay."

Her cheeks were slightly puffed, and her voice sounded annoyed despite her understanding reply. *You don't seem okay with it.*

"Back when we were little, I fell on my butt from the gymnastics bar and started crying, then you said, 'C'mon, that's no reason to cry.' You were doing a back hip circle."

I did?

"Then you did that little rub-rub on my butt. I think that's when I started enjoying those little massages."

"So you're saying you want me to rub your ass?"

"N-nooo! Were you even listening?!"

"It was a joke! Don't get so mad."

"Geez!" she huffed. "Anyway, I don't mind where—I just want you to do your rub-rub."

You don't mind where? So you're saying you would *let me rub your butt. Also, I refuse to ever say "rub-rub." It sounds extra lewd.*

Fushimi noticed the other students around were watching us, and her expression immediately changed.

I had thought Fushimi grew up and stopped being the kid I remembered back in middle school, but after all this time with her lately, so many of those expressions reminded me of when we were kids.

"She's just…pretending at school."

"Did you say something?"

Any other guy would've treasured the memory of the princessly smile she flashed at me, but since I knew it was all an act, it felt more like pressure.

"N-no, nothing."

"I see. Good."

If this were a manga, they would draw a huge SFX sign saying DANGER behind that smile.

Ryou, wanna go have lunch together at the cafeteria?

It was ten minutes before lunch break. Fushimi stealthily scooted her desk next to mine and showed me the message in a corner of her notebook.

Just as I was writing that I already had the lunch Mana made for me, she added an extra note:

Thump-thump

Is that a heart sound effect?!

Sorry. I already brought lunch, so I'll go to the physics room like always, I wrote back.

That appeared to bum her out.

I wasn't against spending lunch with her, but if I did, then the crowds of people trying to get in her good graces would form, and I didn't want to eat lunch with a bunch of noise nearby. Maybe I wouldn't mind it if they were my friends, too, but that wasn't the case.

I want to spend lunch in peace.

With Torigoe?

By myself, I wrote emphatically.

I didn't go to the physics room to be with Torigoe; I did it because no one wouldbother me there.

Fushimi entered hamster-bomb mode, then scooted away.

The bell rang, and just as I'd said, I left for the physics room.

"Takamori," someone called to me.

I turned around, and there was Torigoe, holding a lunch box in her hand.

"Hey, librarian."

"You going to the physics room?"

"Yeah. Like always."

"I figured." She smiled.

We both entered the physics room, then closed the door. That was enough to keep the noise of the school at bay, as if we had entered another world.

I sat at my usual spot and started eating.

We had been together there a couple of times after the day we decided on the committees, but I suddenly wondered why she had volunteered. "Did you want to be class rep?" I asked.

"Not really."

Not really? Then why'd you volunteer?

Surprised, I turned toward her.

She touched her smooth hair on her shoulder, then gave a thoughtful *hmm*. "Well... Um... I just...figured I was kinda close to you, so..."

I had no idea you felt that way, Torigoe... Seems I'm not the only one who feels this kinship.

Torigoe's voice was getting quieter and quieter.

"...So I thought...if some other girl was gonna do it...it might as well be me..."

I see. So you were worried about me...

Thankfully, Fushimi had ended up being my partner, but had it been another girl...like, some other popular, noisy girl, then we would've had trouble understanding each other.

"T-that's all!" she burst out, almost at a shout.

"Wow, thanks for thinking about me."

"...Y-you're welcome." She started shoving food into her mouth: chomp, gulp, chomp, gulp.

Looks like my blind guess about her transcript was totally off the mark.

She asked me about Fushimi then, so I explained everything to her: that

Fushimi was my childhood friend and we hung out a lot when we were little, that we started going our own ways, that something had happened recently that brought us together like old times. I hid nothing from her.

"So that's why you acted like just classmates up until this new year."

"Yup."

"Is it fun being friends with the school princess?"

"More than fun. Feels just like old times. And she acts nothing like a princess when she's with me."

"HRH Fushimi? Un-princess-like? Now that's surprising. But I guess that's how it is with childhood friends."

...She's suddenly awfully chatty. Also, I'm guessing "HRH" means "Her Royal Highness" because she's the princess, or something?

"What do you mean?"

"Since you've known each other for a long time, it's hard for you to be in a romantic relationship. You end up feeling more like family, so you can't see each other that way, right?"

That was the cliché; I'd seen that plenty of times in anime and manga.

However, every time it showed up, I always wondered if it was really the case.

I shook my head. "...Fushimi is smart, she's fit, and she's cute. I've known her basically all my life, and I can perfectly understand why all the boys flock around her."

Although I only noticed she was popular last year.

"And if I can understand them, that means I am seeing her that way."

Being with her is so chill since we've known each other so long. It's fun talking with her about nothing at all and learning bit by bit how she thinks.

It's more common in manga for the protagonist to end up with a heroine who appears later on in his life, instead of the girl who's been by his side from the beginning. After all, if he ended up with the girl who'd always been there, the story wouldn't be as interesting. Too obvious.

...But I don't need my romance to be interesting. I'm fine with boring.

"If we'd stayed close in middle school, maybe I would've noticed much earlier that..." I was confused by what was coming out of my mouth.

H-huh? I would've noticed much earlier that...what? What was I about to say?

"Takamori, your face is red."

"What?! Um, forget it. Just forget I said anything."

"Hmm? Was someone there just now?" Torigoe tilted her head while looking at the door.

"What? I wasn't looking."

"Maybe I'm just seeing things. For a second, I saw the silhouette of a girl in the window."

But there was no trace of any silhouette that I could see.

"...So you like Fushimi, huh, Takamori?"

"Bwuh?! I-I never said anything like that. Why are you asking?"

"'Cause you basically did just now."

I thought she was joking around, but I couldn't hear it in her tone.

"Ryou, that's not the right kanji," Fushimi pointed out while I was writing in the class journal. She taught me the correct character, and I continued.

"What was today's Modern Japanese class about? I remember nothing from first period."

"See, this is why you should write this down right after class ends, so you don't forget."

"...I was asleep."

"Geez, you're such a... Okay, so today we..."

Even with all the scolding, she always helped out and refused to abandon me for being so useless... For now, at least.

She could've gone home without me on the days I was on duty, but she stayed and waited for me to finish writing.

"I'm always worried you'll write something dumb" was her excuse.

"You really are diligent."

"Of course. I'm class rep," she said with a smug smile, adjusting her invisible glasses.

I was still writing in the journal, without further incident, when she stared right at me with a mischievous smile on her face.

"So I heard you see your childhood friend in a romantic way, huh, Ryou?"

The lead of my mechanical pencil broke. "W-what are you talking about?"

"What *am* I talking about, I wonder?" She dodged the question, smiling ear to ear.

During April, PE always focused on fitness tests. We did sidestepping, shuttle runs, long jumps, hundred-meter dashes, and more.

We did all the running and jumping separated by gender, but not even that could stop all the boys—in every year—from watching Fushimi when her turn arrived. Yup, even the third-years were watching us in the field through the windows.

"Hina's amazing…"

"She's so fast…"

I could overhear the girls' conversations.

At the end of every test, we told each other our results.

"Ryou, you're so bad at this," she cheerfully laughed every time.

"I'm not that bad! I'm fifth among the boys, you know. From the bottom."

"Ah-ha-ha. See? You're doing terrible."

"Hey, by my standards, that's pretty good."

Our relationship as old friends and class reps had made the rounds already, so no one gave us strange looks for the friendly chatter. I'd also gotten used to rekindling our friendship again after multiple days of going to and from school together.

"So why won't she join a club?" I heard a girl ask.

That wasn't a surprising question. Not only were her results better than mine, but her total was higher than even those of the track-and-field star and the girls in basketball, tennis, and other sports clubs.

After PE ended, one of our classmates, a girl in a ponytail, came up to me. I recognized her, but I didn't know her name.

"Hey, Prez!"

I took two steps back, worried about my BO after all that exercise. "...I'm just class rep, not president."

"Same difference," she replied. "Anyway, care if I borrow Fushimi?"

"Borrow...? Why ask me? It's not like she's mine."

"I know. I just want your help convincing her. We have the spring tournament coming up next weekend, and we're missing one person to round out the team."

What club is she in again? I wondered while listening to her. Turned out she was in the tennis club.

They would be fine as long as someone new joined the club, but the chances of that were low, and they wouldn't be able to participate in the team matches at this rate.

"You should be asking her yourself..."

"I did, and she turned us down."

Figures. She's in great demand, so if she helped out even one person, she'd never see the end of it.

"Sorry. I can't help you. You're saying you just need to round out the team, right? You don't really need Fushimi in that case, so maybe try asking someone else."

"Oh, don't say that, Prezzz!"

"I'm sure there's tons of other people, like someone in another club or someone who used to do tennis in middle school. And if there aren't, then just write in whoever's name and have someone do double the work the day of the match."

"What, do you think this is some stupid sitcom?"

"It was a joke," I said, laughing, taking back what I'd just said.

There is absolutely no reason why it has to be Fushimi...but this girl does seem to need the help...

"She doesn't even have to buy anything. We'll get her the shoes, the uniform, and the racket! Pretty please?"

It's really hard to turn her down.

Mmm… I groaned, looking for an answer, when I suddenly felt something cold on my back. I shivered and turned around.

"…?"

There's no one there.

"? What's wrong?"

"Nothing." I shook my head. "Okay, I'll ask her. But that's it. I'm not convincing her. I'll just explain the problem, tell her she can come as she is, and leave it all up to her."

"Th-thank you! Yes, that'll work!" She grabbed my hands and shook them with vigor. "Now that's our prez!"

"How many times do I have to tell you I'm not president…?"

And let go of my hands already.

The cold on my back returned, even more intense. I shuddered again.

"Okay, I'm counting on you!"

She waved while leaving, then blew me a kiss. *She must be really happy, huh? I can't handle this type…*

I lazily waved back, then headed to the classroom.

PE was the last class of the day. Everyone was out, going home or at clubs, leaving the classroom empty.

Now, then. Time to write whatever in the journal and go home.

Suddenly, I felt a chill on my neck again and reflexively ducked my head.

What the hell's being going on? Am I sick or something?

"…So you're friends with Honma." Fushimi entered the classroom, her gym uniform neatly folded in her arms.

"Honma? Ah…that tennis girl?"

Wait. The air…the air around me suddenly went subzero!

Fushimi sat at her desk, and the cold worsened even more.

"It's freezing!" I instinctively hugged myself.

©Fly

Fushimi began putting her stuff away while pouting. *Why are you sulking?*

"Not like I mind. It's none of my business who you may or may not be friendly to."

"Sure doesn't seem that way."

"I don't mind."

What's with the low voice?! That's the lowest I've heard her go! Very fitting for this low temperature, I guess!

"A class rep shouldn't hold hands and kiss a girl so out in the open at school. It's scandalous."

"Wait a second! That's not what happened! She grabbed my hands, but that was just a handshake. And we didn't kiss— She just blew one at me."

It was nothing special, considering the context...although I admit both the handshake and the kiss made my heart skip a beat.

Wait, you were watching? So you're why I'm shivering?

"You sure seemed happy, Ryou."

Dammit, I can't deny that. You see, I don't have much experience interacting with girls other than you...

"Class reps should treat all classmates equally, but...this is favoritism."

"It is not," I retorted.

Fushimi finished preparing to go home, but instead, she stayed beside me, grumpy. Apparently, she was waiting for me.

"So are you joining the tennis club? You seemed all fired up and ready to go."

Ah, did she get there halfway through the conversation?

I explained what happened, to resolve the misunderstanding.

"So they want you to help out so they can participate."

"Oh. So that's what it was all about." The cold air started dissipating. "I really...have no choice but to turn them down..."

I get it. Otherwise, they'd never let you free. But I still didn't understand why they were so hell-bent on asking her.

"Want me to let 'em know?"

"No, I'll tell them myself. Thanks."

Fushimi was in a good mood again. As she waited for me to finish writing in the journal, she rested her chin on her hand and stared at me with a smile.

"I can't see how watching me write could be entertaining. Just play with your phone or something."

"No, I'm fine like this."

"You're really nice to me, you know that?"

She helped me out during class and waited for me even though she didn't need to.

"Y-you think so?" Her smile became wider as she giggled.

"But didn't you just say that it's not okay for a class rep to have favo—?"

Fushimi rushed to cut in. "Th-this is childhood-friend privilege! No worries! So... I'd be happy if I could have those privileges, too."

I couldn't help but blush at hearing her say that so close to my face.

"S-sure..." was all I could manage before looking away.

"Ryou, you're red."

"You are too."

Laughs escaped from both of us and echoed in the empty classroom.

Fushimi was restless.

First period was about to end, and she was planning on turning Honma down face-to-face.

I had told her she could just text before class, but she shook her head.

"This kind of thing should be done in person, not over text," she said, going on about good faith or whatever.

She always wanted to do things the right way.

"I'm worried about how she'll react…"

"I doubt she'll hold it against you," I muttered with a glance at Honma, who sat near the front of the class.

The teacher closed the textbook with a thud and declared class over. Fushimi stood up to lead the farewells, and the bell rang, marking the start of a short break.

"Whooooo…"

She took a few deep breaths, like a martial artist preparing for the next match, stood up, and headed over to where Honma was chatting with friends. Fushimi's concern infected me, too, and I watched her with bated breath.

"Ahhh, I figured," Honma said, laughing dejectedly.

The reaction wasn't anything to worry about. What a relief.

"Sorry for turning you down over and over. I'll help you look for someone else."

Fushimi's tone made it clear she was just being considerate. *She should be more honest*, I thought. *You don't have to be so tactful. But I don't know anything about how it is between girls.*

"No, no, it's fine. I'm the one being so adamant."

After all that, she came back with the weary look of someone who'd finished a day of hard work.

"Good thing it all went smoothly."

"Yeah. So next up we have biology… We're moving classrooms, right?"

"We are?"

"Geez. Fine, I'll go ask the teacher."

I tried saying I'd go with her, but she was already gone before I'd even stood up all the way.

I returned to my seat and opened up social media on my phone to pass the time.

"…What is she even busy with? She's not in any club, right?"

"I don't know what she's doing, but…"

"What a bitch. What's wrong with helping out just a bit?"

"She's like antisocial or something. She always goes home early when we ask her to hang out. Like she's a grade-schooler or something."

I lifted my head at the irksome laughter. There I saw Honma with an awkward smile on her face, surrounded by three other sports-club girls.

"Unbelievable. You just asked her to play tennis for one day."

"She's been rude like that since last year. We were in the same class."

I put my phone down on the desk with an audible thud that echoed throughout the entire classroom.

"…Then one of you go to the tournament," I said directly to the people surrounding Honma.

Apparently, my voice carried better than I'd expected—everyone else shut up.

"She just needs one person to round out the team, it doesn't matter who goes."

All three of them were astounded at my sudden interjection.

"It's just 'helping out a bit,' right? ...Don't go assuming people have tons of free time just because they're not in any club. What people do with their time is none of your business."

The classroom was painfully silent compared to the usual break-time chatter.

I came to my senses after hearing the hustle and bustle coming from the hallways.

...This is exactly why I have no friends.

"I'll go ask the teacher if we're moving classrooms now..."

I couldn't bear to stay there any longer, so I excused myself and stood up from my seat.

I turned around and saw Torigoe sitting in the last row, holding her thumb up with her usual inexpressive face. That got a smile out of me, and I headed out the classroom a bit more relaxed.

"...Ah."

"Whoa!" I bumped into Fushimi at the door.

"We're moving classrooms for biology."

"Oh, cool. Okay."

Fushimi slowly entered the silent classroom and wrote **Next class will be in the biology room** on the blackboard. I could tell her hand was trembling.

She must've heard the whole conversation from just outside the classroom. She was waiting for the right moment to come in...

Our classmates grabbed their notebooks and textbooks and left the classroom in a hurry, one after the other, as though escaping from the awkward mood. Soon, there was no one left.

Fushimi turned away from the blackboard.

"I was fine. You didn't have to say all that."

"Don't lie."

It's obvious it affected you. Anyone would be shocked hearing someone talk behind their back.

"I'm used to it."

"Please don't get used to that."

"Everyone will blame you for it."

"I don't care. It's not like anyone has a good opinion of me anyway."

"Ah-ha-ha," she laughed painfully, trying to not make me worry.

"Don't force yourself to laugh."

"No... I have to...or I'll cry." Tears were already welling up in her eyes. *Too late.*

I said nothing; instead, I rubbed her hair. She rested her head on my shoulder and sniffled.

"Ryou... Thank you."

Looks like both class reps are gonna be late to next period.

"Hee-hee. How cute…"

I was lying on my bed, playing with my handheld console, with Fushimi sprawled beside me, giggling. She held one of my manga volumes.

"Are you having fun?"

"Yes, it's very fun!"

Cool.

Once she found out I liked manga, Fushimi asked me for recommendations, one of which she was now reading. It was a rom-com for boys, so I wasn't sure she'd like it, but apparently I was wrong.

I could occasionally hear her reacting with a little "Ooh" or "Wow!" while she read, leisurely fluttering her legs.

I gave her a sidelong glance, and all I could see was her pure-white thighs. I hurriedly looked away, lifted my hips, and distanced myself a bit.

"Who do you think is the cutest?" she asked.

"I think that'd be Karin."

"Oh, very understandable."

"She's cute."

Karin was one of the heroines: the one who liked the protagonist from the beginning.

There were barely any serious moments in the story, which was one of its selling points—it was an easy read.

"Next, next!" Fushimi demanded. She had already finished the fourth volume and was rushing right into the fifth. Now she was twisting and turning, flopping from faceup to facedown to faceup again, restlessly try-ing to find the optimal posture.

"I think it's best to just use a chair and desk," I commented. A fact a manga newbie like her wouldn't know.

"Hmm... Let's see... Like this..." She moved, still lying faceup. "Oh, this feels right."

I was sitting cross-legged, and she took the chance to rest her head on my knee.

"Oh... Please don't let me interfere with your gaming. Enjoy your-self," she said while glancing back at the manga.

What kind of enjoyment am I supposed to get out of this?

"Your head is too heavy."

"C'mon—just for a bit."

Geez, fine... Oh? Her skirt's hemline was farther up her leg than usual, most likely because she was bending her knees. This part of her thighs was not used to seeing the light of day.

Gulp.

Considering her lazy posture, the slightest breeze would flip it up.

"Fushimi... Um, your skirt... I can almost see...y'know."

She rested the open manga on her slim chest, then swiftly pulled her skirt down, returning it to its position six inches above her knees.

Her face was slightly red.

"Ryou...you pervert."

"I'm not— I just warned you..."

Fushimi stared at me with a serious look on her face. "Ryou, have you ever wanted to see a girl's panties, too?"

There was a scene like that in that manga. Nothing too excessive, though—the kind of just slightly naughty scene that's still firmly PG.

"Never." *Yes, I would die for it.*

"I see... What about if I offered?"

For real?

"…No."

"Hee-hee. I only asked because I knew you'd say that."

I can't tell if she really trusts me or thinks I'm just that pathetic.

Fushimi grabbed the manga again and went back to reading. Soon enough, her hemline was drifting north again.

For heaven's sake…

Her thighs were taking attention away from my gaming.

"I'll go get some juice."

"Huh? No, don't worry about that."

"I said I'm going." I took her pillow away as I moved my knee and stood up, then left the room.

"Haaah…"

When did my bedroom turn into an endurance test chamber?

I could feel the MP fading away from my body.

When I got to the kitchen, I took a good breath of fresh air and poured the juice. Then I went back to my room.

"I brought apple juice again. That okay?"

"Whaaa…?! A-ahhh, yes!"

Fushimi was no longer holding my manga; as soon as I entered the room, she rocketed over to the bed and sat on her knees.

"?"

"…"

Our eyes met, and she immediately turned away. She cleared her throat, then took a more relaxed sitting posture.

Her face is…a little stiff?

She hid her lips in her mouth, then took her tongue out ever so slightly to moisten them.

"Are you thirsty? You should've said so, geez," I said, giving her one of the glasses I'd brought.

"Th-thanks…"

Our fingers touched when she took it, making my heart skip a beat.

"S-sorry…"

"N-no, don't worry…"

Well, this is awkward.

Fushimi gulped down the whole glass of juice.

I felt too awkward sitting with her on the bed again, so I decided to game from my chair.

I put my glass down on the desk and noticed something unusual—a thin, square packet the size of my palm. A circle was jutting out from within the square.

Is this a…a love glove?! Where did this come from?!

I doubt this is something for school, asking me to measure the circle's area or something.

The wrapping had **Do it right, Bubby** ♡ written in Mana's handwriting.

That damn gyaru! Get out of my business! When did this thing even get here…?

Has it…been here from the beginning and I didn't notice…?

And Fushimi saw it after I left…?

"…I'll get back to reading…" She sat upright with the manga in her hands.

It's upside down!

I can tell that thing has you flustered! You're redder than the reddest tomato!

She didn't point it out and call me a pervert like just a few minutes before. Now she was simply too embarrassed to even crack a joke. This wasn't light, silly lewdness like panties or whatever—this was *serious business.*

Her breathing was heavy as she tried to fan her redness away with her hand.

"F-Fushimi."

"Huh?! Yeah?!"

I could hear her gulping all the way from where I was.

"I-I'll lend you the manga. I—I just remembered I have something to do."

"I—I—I see."

"Y-y-yeah."

"O-okay then, I-I'll go home!"

I packed all the volumes up to the latest one in a bag.

It was already dark outside, so I decided to walk her home.

We stepped outside in silence, with a palpable air of tension around us.

Awkward...

Yeah, who wouldn't panic after seeing that without any warning? Hell, I'm panicking right now.

Once her house entered our sights, she said she'd go the rest of the way alone and took the bag of manga.

"Sure. Okay, see you tomorrow."

I turned my back to her and started away, when I heard her yell, "R-Ryou!"

She was peeking out of her house's door, as if it was some sort of shield.

"What is it?"

"...I-I'm not okay with doing that kind of thing without going through the proper procedures first! Y-you idiot!" She fled into her house and shut the door.

"I—I didn't even ask for it...!" I tried explaining, but she was already gone.

"Dammit, Mana..." I aggressively scratched my head in frustration before going back home.

...Although, she didn't call me a pig or a jerk or disgusting.

I thought back on what she'd just said, and I turned around to her house.

The lights in Fushimi's room on the second floor were on. Her curtains were open, and a figure appeared in the window, waving a hand.

I waved back.

Fushimi...

The way you said that makes it sound as if you would be okay with doing it if we did go through the proper procedures first, you know?

Nah... I'm overthinking it.

The evidence was overwhelming, so I cross-examined the obvious culprit.

"You're the oldest son of the Takamori house—you have to be careful," Mana pleaded.

Her face was as serious as could be, but everything else about the matter seemed poorly planned.

Also, I thought *she* needed to be more cautious, too.

"Takamoriii, should we go to the gym for the next class?" a girl called out to me during our short break between classes.

"Yeah, if I recall correctly."

"Thankies," she replied before leaving.

Fwoom...!

Hellfire blew from behind Fushimi in the seat next to me.

"...Wait, was I wrong? We're not going to the gym?"

"No... You're right."

Why's your voice so low?! It sounded like it was coming from the very depths of hell! Why are you so upset if I was right?!

"She could've asked me instead of you. I'm much better informed," she muttered and huffed.

During lunch, I told Torigoe about it in the physics room.

"That reaction...makes it way too obvious...," she replied vaguely.

We were sitting far away from each other as always, but I could still hear her quiet voice thanks to our noiseless surroundings.

"I think maybe they find it easier to ask me," I said. "Fushimi can be really serious, while I'm more relaxed."

"I get that feeling. Girls do have this sort of...hierarchy. Fushimi's at the top, so she may not understand," she explained. "It's kinda intimidating. So it is easier to talk to someone more relaxed, like you. If she's the princess, naturally us plebs will find it easier to speak to an attendant raised along the common folk, wouldn't we?"

I guess?

"So is it the same for you, then?" I asked. "Do you find it easier talking with me than with other girls?"

"Sometimes the opposite sex is easier to approach. Boys are excluded from the Class B girls' hierarchy."

"Huh."

Fushimi was at the cafeteria with some classmates today, too. Still pretending.

Wonder what the deal with those blue flames was, I thought.

"There's also the effects of the Fushimi buff," Torigoe added.

"The what buff?"

"Since Fushimi has such a good time talking to you, it makes you more attractive to the other girls."

I do not understand women...

The conversation ended, and Torigoe took her chopsticks to start eating.

"You've got a good handle on what people are thinking—does that mean you feel the same way?"

"Koff, koff!" Torigoe choked up.

"Are you okay?"

"Wh-what kind of question is that?" She opened her plastic bottle and gulped down some of her tea.

"Well, I just noticed that you're really observant."

"I don't exactly think about it that much..." Her face was red, probably from the choking.

Surely she saw us quite a bit, what with her sitting behind us.

Torigoe tried clearing her throat until she finally calmed down. "…Anyway, you have the Fushimi buff now. Do you know what that means?"

"That people have an easier time talking to me, right?"

Torigoe tilted her head—guess my answer wasn't quite right. "Not really, but not too far off the mark. I'll give you sixty points."

Are we playing riddles now or something?

"Let's say there's a sheep."

"Wait, why are we talking about sheep now?"

"Just one sheep, which has one wolf after it."

"Um, Torigoe?"

"Then we have other wolves who know this sheep and come to the conclusion that it must taste pretty good if it's got another wolf after it."

Is this like a fable or something…?

"Got it?"

What am I even supposed to get? What are you talking about? And don't look at me like it's so obvious.

Suddenly, someone opened the door, and Fushimi appeared.

"…Ryou, we need a world map for history class in fifth period. Help me out?"

Oh yeah, the teacher did say that.

"Sure," I replied. I was already done with lunch, so I packed my stuff.

I left the physics room without saying anything and headed for the world-history storeroom with Fushimi. She already had the key with her, and her grumpy mood was gone now.

"I read all the manga you lent me."

"Cool. What did you think?"

"It was fun. The girls were all cute."

I was worried she wouldn't like it, so that was good to hear.

"Although…" She pouted. "Karin ended up not doing much. I didn't like that."

That isn't uncommon in pure rom-coms. Heroines in love with the protagonist show up one after the other, and after you've learned the guy's backstory and how all the other girls feel, Karin ends up seeming like a bystander.

"But you said she was cute."

"Yeah. I like her, and that's why I want her to win. But then..."

"Well, she said it herself. She cares about him, so she decided that staying away would be for the best. Or something like that."

"That's just an excuse."

RIP, Karin. Fushimi attacked with the fierceness of an Internet comment section.

We reached the history room, and Fushimi inserted the key to open the door.

"She's trying to act like the bigger person by admitting defeat despite her feelings. Being the tragic heroine sucks." Fushimi sniffled, and tears were welling up in her eyes as she opened the door and stepped inside. "How many volumes are there?"

"It's still being published. There's ten volumes now, so I think it'll keep going for a bit more."

I answered while I searched for the map, which I found right away. It was too big to carry alone.

"There's nothing good about having to hide your feelings, having to stop yourself from confessing them."

She really got into Karin's character, huh?

"I would... If that were me, I wouldn't give up on my love," she declared, staring straight at me. "Is it not enough for her to be always there for him? To be cute and stay out of trouble? I can't stand it... I hate that the childhood friend always loses to some other girl who shows up later..."

I don't remember her character quite being the typical childhood friend, but I guess that's what she is.

"Okay, okay, calm down. It's just manga."

"You're right," she replied in a tone that suggested I was not right.

I didn't want to spend the entire trip back to the classroom in silence, so I asked, "So what was up with the hellfire earlier?"

"Um, what?"

"Ah, I mean, not literally, but right before PE something seemed to be burning you."

"Ahhh… That…" She closed her mouth and thought for a while before looking in my general direction and asking, "Ryou…do you ever get annoyed when I'm talking with other boys?"

We'd been in the same class for our entire lives, so I'd seen her talking with other guys since we were in grade school.

"I can't remember feeling like that, no."

Fushimi scowled and puffed her cheeks. "…Then I'm not telling you!"

"…What?"

Fushimi softened her expression and laughed.

"Ryou, Ryou, are you free today?"

"You must've noticed by now I'm free most days."

"Nice. So wanna go to karaoke?"

"Karaoke? Uh, yeah, sure."

Now that was unexpected. Fushimi didn't usually say she wanted to go somewhere after school.

After classes were done and we reached the station closest to our houses, I understood.

There were five students wearing uniforms different from ours right there at the ticket gate. Two girls and three boys.

"Oh, so that's what's going on…"

"What is it?" Fushimi turned her head around.

Yeah. She never said it would be just the two of us. I should've asked.

It'd be awkward to take it back now that we're here…

Fushimi joined the five and greeted her old friends from middle school.

"It's been so long!"

"How've you been?"

They're having so much fun… I can't rain on their parade now!

I followed her lead and greeted them. I did recognize the three dudes, but they weren't my friends or anything.

"Hey, it's like a class reunion here!" one of the girls called, and everyone reacted in kind, while I sighed internally. Externally, though, I agreed with my best fake smile.

I could already guess they'd insisted on bringing Fushimi, and she hadn't had it in her to turn them down. She didn't seem the type to enjoy karaoke.

We headed to the place right next to the station, and they bombarded Fushimi with questions on our way there. How school was going, whether she'd joined any clubs, whether she had a boyfriend, etc. She responded with her faux princess smile.

Our marching formation was three-three-one. Fushimi was at the center of the front line, while I was the one at the back.

We entered the building, set the time we'd spend there at the desk, and were guided to our room.

Fushimi called to me, a faint smile on her face. "Ryou, can you even sing?"

"Oh, please. I come here all the time with Mana."

"Really? Wow."

..."All the time" in reality meant "a couple of times a year."

"How about you?"

"I'm...pretty average."

Average, eh? That could mean anything. She seems quite confident, though.

We poured our drinks at the soda fountain before entering the room, then picked our songs one by one.

Everyone picked popular recent songs or idol songs everybody knew, pumping up each singer in turn by clapping or shaking maracas.

"What're you singing, Ryou?" Fushimi, forgetting all about her princessly act, peeked at the tablet in my hands while I was choosing.

"Bubby, let me teach you about my hidden special move."

"Uh, are we still talking about karaoke?"

"You can never go wrong with anime songs. Just choose one you used to watch if you're with people your age. You'll have them in the palm of your hand!"

"How can you always be so right...?"

"Make sure to choose one that shows animation. It'll get everyone excited, and their attention will be on the screen instead of your singing. And if someone starts singing even without a mic, give them one."

"I am so fortunate to be able to bask in your wisdom..."

Heh. Finally, the time to put Mana's theory to the test had arrived.

"Oh, you'll see." I chose the song without letting Fushimi see. The title showed on the screen, but no one realized what it was.

Fushimi's turn came before mine.

I didn't recognize it from the title, but I got it as soon as the intro started: It was a ballad from a certain singer-songwriter who'd become popular the previous year.

I could tell everyone was listening attentively. Her voice was powerful yet pleasant; you'd hardly guess she could sing like this from her normal speaking tone.

I listened carefully in silence, too.

Once she finished, she said, "Your turn, Ryou," then gave me the mic.

"...Y-yeah..."

"Hina, you're so good!"

"Fushimi, that was badass!"

The others flooded her with praise.

Yeah, it was so good you'd think she's taking classes or something. Color me surprised.

But...now I don't want to sing. Aghhh!

You should've told me you'd choose a song like that, man! I'm supposed to follow a soft ballad with an anime song?!

Sorry, guys, hope you enjoyed the mood while it lasted.

God... I shouldn't have rushed to take Mana's advice...

I checked that the mic was on and cleared my throat.

My worry ended up being for nothing. All the guys reached max hype levels the second the animation started playing; anime songs resonated much more deeply with them than girly romantic ballads, it seemed.

The girls only went "Oh, I know that one," but the boys' excitement was enough to prove Mana's theory right.

Thanks to the hype factor, nobody paid attention to my not-bad, not-good singing. *Nice, nice.*

We did a couple more rounds, until two of the girls stood up to go to the restroom.

We took that as a break, so I grabbed my now empty cup and headed for the soda fountain.

"You're not bad at all, Ryou," Fushimi said with a smile, following me.

"Nothing special either, though."

"Sorry for not telling you about who else was coming."

"It's fine. It's also my fault for not asking."

I was anxious at first, but my efforts picking the song were rewarded by the boys' excitement.

"Hina's so good at singing, don't you think?" I heard one of the girls say from the corner of the hall, near the restroom.

"But why did she bring Takamori? We're not three and three anymore."

"She said she wouldn't come otherwise."

"I see... Gotta say, though, picking anime songs was a terrible choice."

"Yeah, like, get a clue, man."

"Ah-ha-ha," they giggled together.

The smile faded away from Fushimi's face.

Ah, well, now I know what being the target of murderous rage feels like. She certainly seems poised to kill.

She took a step toward the hallway, so I immediately grabbed her arm.

"Don't mind them. It's fine. I'm sure they weren't trying to be mean... Hey, c'mere!"

She wrenched her arm out of my grip, then stomped her way to the corner.

"Oh, Hina..."

"Are there any rules about picking songs in karaoke or something?"

I could tell just from her voice how furious she was.

What about your princess act…?

"Huh? You're scaring me. What's wrong?"

"The boys had a good time with it, right? Ryou doesn't need to get a clue—he's doing it on purpose."

The girls didn't have a reply for that.

"…Sorry. I'm going home," Fushimi snapped, her face still twisted in anger. "Ryou, let's go."

"We still have time left, y'know?"

"I don't care anymore."

"Well, I guess the princess has to follow her whims."

It didn't seem as if anything would convince her to stay, so I didn't try.

Fushimi gave our part of the bill to the boys still in the room, then we grabbed our bags and left. I tried paying her, but she wouldn't take it.

As stubborn as ever, eh? And now she's walking faster than usual. She never changes.

"I told you, they weren't trying to be mean. They're just playing around…"

"Still, that's not okay." She was still angry; her pout was the pout to end all pouts. "Sorry… I thought we'd have some fun since we used to be classmates, but that was the opposite of what I'd hoped."

"Don't be. I had fun singing and listening."

"Really? I'm glad, then."

"You should've left them alone. There was no need to get in an argument for me…"

"I wanted to. You did the same thing for me when they were talking behind my back, remember?"

"Yeah, but it doesn't matter who I get in a fight with. No one cares about me either way."

"That's not true. Why do you put yourself down like that?"

Why? I don't know.

My old friend stared at me the whole way home.

"…Y'know, you *are* cool, Ryou."

"Please don't say that to my face."

No one had ever told me that; I didn't know how to react.

"Well, I guess I'm the only one who needs to know. Hee-hee," she said, giggling. Her expressions really were all over the place.

"Let's go just the two of us next time."

"That'd be fine, I guess."

"Yes!"

Fushimi cheered up as we approached her house.

©Fly

Saturday had arrived, and I had whatever for breakfast before getting ready to go out. The skies were clear; the chance of rain was zero for the whole day. Perfect day to go outside.

"..." Mana stared at me from a corner of the room.

"...What?"

"Where are you going?"

"Going for a stroll at Hamadani."

Hamadani was the biggest shopping district around. There was a mall, as well as enough fun spots to spend a whole day there.

I was ignoring Mana's stare while I changed when I got a text from Fushimi.

I just left my house!

Which meant she'd be there in around five minutes.

"Bubby, that outfit... Don't tell me you've got a date?"

"No. I'm just going with Fushimi."

"Sounds like a date to me."

"I said no." I got changed, then checked to make sure I wasn't missing anything before I left my room.

"Whoo. Nice outfit, Bubby." Mana gave me a thumbs-up.

'Course it is. It's the outfit you recommended to me a while ago.

"I am such a fashion genius," she added.

"Awfully proud of yourself, huh?"

I went downstairs, and Mana followed me, purportedly intending to see me off. The doorbell rang just as we approached, so Mana opened the door.

"Hi, Hina!"

"Oh, Mana. Morning."

They greeted each other with a smile.

"...Hina."

"Yes?" Fushimi tilted her head while Mana studied her whole figure, up and down. Fushimi didn't pay my sister much attention, instead leaning over and waving at me behind her.

"Hey, Bubby, c'mere." Mana turned around with a grim expression. "Is that really Hina?"

"Can't you see? She even answered your greeting just now."

"Don't you think her outfit's kinda wild?"

Wild? I doubt she'd wear anything too gaudy.

I curiously peered at Fushimi over Mana's shoulder.

"...Yeah, that is wild."

She was wearing a T-shirt featuring some weird character, like a barely known local mascot or something, and a frilly skirt like you'd see on a much younger girl.

Is this some sort of joke? Is she waiting for me to deliver her punch line?

I knew nothing about girls' clothes, and even I realized that this was kinda wild.

"Bubby, what is going on? How can this be the taste of such a beautiful teenage girl?!"

"W-wait, maybe it's so tacky it's actually..."

"No way in hell. If anything, it goes beyond ironically good back to being bad again."

"I know what you're getting at, and...yeah. This is indefensible."

"If she says she meant to do this, I will pass out on the floor." Mana's eyes opened wide, as if she'd just had an epiphany. "She's trying to make you laugh, Bubby. That has to be it. There's no way anyone would wear such an ugly T-shirt for non-comedic purposes."

"Y-you think so?"

"You can't leave her hanging. Give the poor girl a reaction."

While we were whispering to each other, Fushimi asked, as if nothing was wrong, "What's the matter?"

Mana pointed at her with her chin. I nodded.

"Um, uh, your clothes... You've got good taste, huh?"

"Oh, really?!" Her eyes sparkled as she gleefully turned around 360 degrees. "I'm sooo glad! I was thinking about what to wear the whole night. Hee-hee." She bashfully smiled.

"Yeah, you're a comedy genius! Bravo, bravo! It's hilarious!" I clapped like I'd just heard a rousing orchestra performance.

"Huh...?"

"All right, now change into your real clothes and let's get going."

Tears welled up in her eyes. "I...I tried really hard...choosing what to wear..."

T-minus five seconds to bawling!

Now what, Mana?! It wasn't a joke!

I turned toward my sister, but she wasn't there. She was on the floor, her eyes rolled back into her head.

"Th-this is...the fashion sense...of the prettiest girl in town..."

"Manaaaaaaa!"

"It's...so ugly..."

No, don't say that out loud!

"!!!" Fushimi was legitimately shocked— She crouched down right there on the floor. "It's not a jooooooooke!"

Our plans for a day on the town went out the window after that carnage.

I took Mana and Fushimi to my room after the former came to and the latter calmed down.

"Is this all you've got?" The fashion police kicked off the interrogation.

"It's the best one I have, but I do own more, like..." Fushimi listed all her clothing that she thought was fashionable.

Mana's expression turned grimmer and grimmer with every article. "This was a hopeless case from the beginning..."

"Don't say that!" Fushimi cried.

"I'll burn that cursed closet on sight."

"No, don't!"

Mana breathed a deep sigh. "I hear Bubby's going on his first date, and whaddaya know—it's with Hina. 'So far, so good,' I thought."

"Hey, i-it's not my first."

"Don't lie. I know it is."

...*It is.*

...*How do you know?*

Fushimi finally broke her dejected silence then. "I've never bought my own clothing... I always just use whatever I have at home..."

"What have you been doing since middle school?"

"I always say no when it's on weekends."

"Uh-huh. So you've only gone out in your school uniform."

"Yes," she said, nodding.

Mana must've felt for her— She stood up. "Fine. I'll lend you my clothes!"

"Are you sure...?"

"Yeah! Bubby likes my style anyway, so that's two birds with one stone!"

Fushimi squinted at me suspiciously.

"No, that's not true! That's not my thing! Where is this info even coming from?"

"C'mon—let's go," Mana said, taking Fushimi's hand and leading her to her room.

"First, take off that T-shirt. It's ugly as sin."

"You don't have to be so rude about it..."

"Pretty small boobs you have there, Hina."

"I'm quite aware, thank you."

I could hear them happily quipping at each other from my room.

I don't think gyaru *fashion would fit Fushimi, but I guess we'll see.*

"You also need some makeup."

"I have makeup on!"

"No, no. I mean makeup that goes with your clothes. It all needs to be matching. Cohesive."

"...Okay."

Mana would suggest something, Fushimi would refuse, and then Mana would refuse the refusal. Despite the back and forth, they sounded as if they were having fun.

"There! Perfect!"

"O-ohhhh?!"

What? What's happening?

I peeked at the hallway, and just then, the door opened, letting Mana out.

Fushimi was hiding behind her, so Mana had to pull her forward.

She had on a sexy lace (I think?) top that was slightly transparent around the collarbone and arms, and a skirt with a floral pattern.

"So? So? How's my makeover, Bubby? Fashionable and cute!" Mana made Fushimi turn around in a circle.

I could see an entire third of her back. The sexiness made my heart skip a beat.

Her long hair was now in a wave with a little fluff to it.

"What do you think, Ryou?"

"I—I think...it's incredible."

"Yes!" She hopped and high-fived Mana.

Fushimi was already pretty, so this only elevated what was already there. I had seen those clothes many times before, since they were Mana's, but they gave a different impression on Fushimi.

The poser *gyaru* look she'd had during middle school wasn't quite right, but this fit her amazingly. It wasn't nearly so aggressive—Mana had meticulously adjusted the style to suit her.

"But, Mana, isn't my bra showing…?"

"It's fine, it's fine. Let 'em see that baby."

"N-no!" Fushimi blushed and kept turning to show Mana different angles. "How is it? Can you see it?"

"I'm telling you, Bubby's gonna be a fan."

"…"

"He always tells me to stop when I do it, but I know he loves it."

"Huh?" Fushimi's voice was low. She looked at me as if I were trash left out on the street.

"I—I do not!"

Mana cackled. "Let's go buy some clothes together sometime. I'll give you more advice then."

"Yeah. Thanks, Mana."

Mana's been playing with her since she was little, too, so they're also childhood friends, now that I think about it.

"Let's go, Ryou."

"Ah, yeah."

Maybe the change was just unfamiliar, but I felt as if the girl at my side wasn't Fushimi. I couldn't tell whether it was fresh or just unsettling.

Her exposed white skin and flashes of shoulder blade were really sexy, though.

Oh my God! I can see her bra when she leans over!

I quickly looked away so she wouldn't be able to tell I'd seen it.

And so the fashionable Fushimi and I left my house one hour later than planned.

"I want to make up for what happened at karaoke," Fushimi had told me, and we'd agreed on going out that weekend.

I didn't really mind what had happened at karaoke, but she did.

I told you again and again not to worry...

After Fushimi's makeover at the hands of a true-blue expert, we took the train to the shopping district.

"Are those also Mana's high heels?"

"Yeah. Good thing she's the same size as me!"

Come to think of it, they were also around the same height.

We walked through the towering business buildings as we headed to the mall.

"Your clothes are pretty great, Ryou. Yeah...this is nice," she said as she observed me up and down and back.

My clothes had also been sponsored by Mana, and thankfully they turned out to be in line with Fushimi's taste. My average, boring self passed the test of her high-class eyes.

Fushimi was walking beside me with a skip in her step when something in a show window caught her attention. There was a mannequin wearing seasonal clothing.

"Wanna go inside?"

"No... I was just wondering...how other people are seeing us."

"Who knows? Like some friends out having fun?"

Fushimi's cheeks puffed. "Yeah, I guess." Then she hastily moved along.

"Are you sulking?"

"No."

Yeah, she totally is.

I found an ice-cream stand and bought a cup of soft-serve. "...Want some?"

"I do!"

Fushimi was immediately back in a good mood. I could almost see the stars in her eyes.

Now I know she still loves sweets.

I gave her the cup and spoon. She smiled in pure joy as she took a bite and then another.

I saw a bench nearby, so we sat down.

"Here you go, Ryou." She'd scooped a spoonful of ice cream, and she held it out to me.

...This is the same spoon she's been using, right? I didn't get an extra.

"..."

Th-th-that's an indirect kiss!

But wait. If I turn her down...would she think I'm afraid of an indirect kiss?

I—I do this with Mana all the time, so it's not a big deal.

"S-sure. Here, lemme..."

I tried taking the spoon, but:

"No, no." She shook her head, a serious look on her face.

"Open your mouth."

"Huh?"

"Open. Say 'ah.' Quick, it's gonna melt."

That's a whole level beyond an indirect kiss!

"H-hurry up...," she muttered, her cheeks turning red.

Don't do it if you're embarrassed about it! You're just gonna make it worse for me.

"We shouldn't be doing this in pu—*glup*."

She shoved the spoon into my mouth.

"Is it good?"

"Yeah…"

"Good." Her smile was dazzling.

I wasn't about to have her spoon-feed me any more after that, so I took only occasional bites while she kept the spoon all to herself.

"So do you have a plan in mind for today?"

"A plan? Y-yes, I do."

"What is it?"

"It's a secret."

Why?

Fushimi pattered her feet while sitting on the bench, humming. Even her humming was masterful.

Maybe it was that I wasn't used to seeing her like this, but—her behavior struck me as so sweet…cute, even.

…No, it's not because she's been dressed by a fashion expert now. It's only because this side of her comes as a surprise to me—that's it.

"You've been staring at me this whole time. You really do like *gyarus*, don't you, Ryou?"

"I'm telling you, that was just something I made up so they wouldn't make fun of me. I don't like them."

How many times must I repeat myself?

Fushimi giggled. "No, it's fine. If that's the case, I'll get Mana to teach me about the cutting edge of city fashion."

My chest was pounding hard. Was it because she never acted this way at school? Was it just having this all-new Fushimi sit next to me? I didn't quite know.

After we finished the ice cream, we entered a huge commercial building. There were designer shops, a theater, and everything from general stores to restaurants. The place was full of people, old and young.

Fushimi stared at the floor map, then said, "Oh, we can watch movies here."

"Are there any that catch your eye? Wanna watch one?"

"Yeah, let's go!"

We made our way through the gigantic building, which was as big as a dungeon.

We got to the theater, and Fushimi said she wanted to watch an American action movie.

Thank God she didn't choose a sad romance or something... I've never cried at those.

We bought the tickets and, once it was time, entered the cinema.

"Hey, Fushimi, you sure about paying for the tickets?"

She said she wanted it to be on her, since the purpose of our outing was to apologize.

"It's fine. Otherwise, it wouldn't be an apology, would it?"

I told her I didn't need any apology in the first place, but she didn't listen. *You stubborn, fastidious goofball.*

Okay then, I'll accept it.

I put my hand on the armrest and felt something smooth.

Hmm? What's this soft sensation?

"!!!"

I turned to look at what I was touching. It was a hand.

Fushimi was beet red, her mouth in the shape of a V.

She's blinking beyond light speed! She must be really upset!

"Sorry, this wasn't my armrest..."

"Th-th-this one's m-mine!"

"Y-y-y-y-yeah!"

Th-that almost made my heart burst out of my chest...

I grabbed...her hand...

"!!"

Fushimi closed her eyes tight, still blushing all the way up to her ears and clutching her hand close to her chest.

Now it's making me blush, too. I've been in a panic all day. Maybe because I never go out with her like this?

The place turned dark, and the movie started.

It was a pretty normal Hollywood flick: There was action, a love story, and the protagonist beat the bad guys at the end, then got together with the heroine. It was as cliché as cliché went, but watching the big action set pieces in the theater with that explosive sound drew you into the story.

The credits ended, and everyone started leaving their seat.

"That was fun!"

"Yeah. Theaters are great, huh?"

"Right? It's totally different from watching it at home."

"I thought the same. This genre, especially, is much better at the theater."

"Agreed!"

For a second, I was surprised at how similar our tastes were, then I realized it should be obvious. We always watched the same anime when we were little, then had our parents take us to watch the films together— it was only natural that we'd have similar preferences.

All the other spectators had finally left the theater, and the staff had started cleaning up the place.

We left our seats, too. The back of my hand brushed against Fushimi's as we walked together.

My heart skipped a beat, and I instinctively drew my hand away. Or tried to.

My hand didn't move.

Because Fushimi's left hand was gently holding my fingers.

I couldn't tell what she meant by doing that, even though I could usually tell what she was thinking after so many years together.

I was about to ask her what was the matter, but she talked first, her cheeks flushed.

"C-can I…do this for the rest of the day…?"

I could feel Fushimi's warmth as she held my right hand.

What should I answer...? She means she wants to hold my hand for the entire day, right?

H-how are we supposed to go to the bathroom?!

My mind was going crazy thinking about how that could even work, when:

"W-wait, I have to go to the restroom." She let my hand go and walked right to the bathroom.

Y-yeah. Obviously, she'd let go if she wanted to go...

I leaned on the wall and sighed. Yes. I wanted to say yes, but I panicked. More than anything, I wanted to ask why, but I couldn't summon the courage for that, either.

Isn't that kind of thing only for couples? She wants to hold my hand even though we're not going out?

I surveyed the area and saw many couples here and there.

They were holding hands or gently locking arms. Normal couple stuff.

"..."

The mere thought of us doing something similar set my brain on fire.

I was lucky that she gave me some time alone. Otherwise, I would've overheated and been unable to say anything for the rest of the day. I put my hands in my coat's pockets and found a Band-Aid inside one of them.

"What's up with this?"

I didn't remember putting it there...or having a plan to use one. Maybe Mana was the culprit again.

Is she worried I'll trip and graze a knee or something?

Fushimi came back while I was trying to figure out the mystery.

"Sorry for making you wait," she said. "Let's go."

Oh, she's acting pretty normal.

I started walking, and Fushimi followed right by my side.

I glanced at my hand, but she didn't try anything similar again.

Is she not doing it...because I didn't answer?

Agh, I don't get it. I usually understand what she's thinking at school or on our way home, but now...

She said she wanted to eat something sweet just as we got into the elevator, so we looked at the guide and got off at the floor that had all the restaurants.

"Ryou, do you like sweets?"

"Yeah."

"You haven't changed, huh?" She giggled.

We entered a café, and normalcy finally returned. Once we got to our seats, we talked about school, our work as class reps, and where we should go next.

...It was all normal. She was acting exactly like the Fushimi I knew.

Once we finished our cakes (the cheapest on the menu) after an hour or so, we left the café.

"Are you sure you don't like *gyarus*, Ryou?"

"How many times must I answer the same question? I don't."

"So...you didn't like the clothes I borrowed from Mana for today." She seemed a bit dejected.

Oh, is that what she meant?

"They look good on you."

"Hee-hee. Good to know."

Why is it that praising her directly takes so much brain energy?

Afterward, we looked around a fashionable boutique, and a cute member of the staff caught my eye.

"I see. So I should be wearing clothes like these…"

She took that as indication that she should study the woman's style.

Fushimi's fashion sense was only as awful as it was because she never went out with friends, so it should get a bit more reasonable if she started studying.

"I have to consult with Miss Mana."

Mana was a great cook, responsible, and fashionable, so she was quite knowledgeable despite dressing like a rebel.

"I don't get why she doesn't have a boyfriend," I commented.

"Ryou…you don't know…?" She seemed appalled.

"Huh? Know what?"

"Nothing, forget it."

Fushimi looked away, then grabbed a dress that seemed to have caught her attention and turned to a mirror to see if it would work on her.

"It would look amazing on you!" The attendant I'd glanced at earlier approached and called out to her.

"Huh? Ah, y-yeah…? You t— I mean, thanks."

Heh, I heard that little slip.

"Let me know if you'd like to try it on, too."

"Th-thank you." Fushimi was anxious.

I understood that feeling. I'd be nervous myself if someone suddenly started talking to me.

The attendant smiled at her, as if she were peacefully watching over a kitten. "So you're here today with your brother?"

"…"

Fushimi's eyes rolled back into her head! Why must the most beautiful die so soon?!

"Hey, Fushimi, don't leave us!" I shook her shoulders, and she regained consciousness.

"Ah... I just had a dream... Where someone mistook us for brother and sister."

It wasn't a dream.

I guess it was too much for her brain, and she short-circuited?

The attendant realized her error and forced a smile. "Please take your time," she said in an especially high pitch, then hurriedly left.

Fushimi kept studying herself in the mirror with that dress she liked.

I checked the tag on another one of the same kind. It was 3,000 yen.

...So I'm guessing she wants it, but she can't afford it after paying for my movie ticket.

I took a picture and sent it to Mana. She immediately replied, it's so cute!

"Ryou, what do you think?" Fushimi turned around, holding on to the dress.

I thought she'd look good in pretty much anything... Well, anything not totally bizarre like the outfit she wore to my house this morning.

I wasn't sure about how correct my opinion would be, but considering Mana also said it was cute, I could have some confidence.

"I think it looks good."

"I see, I see. Okay," she said as she folded it and put it back in its place.

"You don't want it?"

"Mmm... Not today."

"What size do you need? Is this one okay?"

"Yes, but...what? Why?"

"In honor of our first outing together after a hundred years...I'll gift it to you."

"What?! No, I'm fine!" she argued, but I didn't pay her any attention and took the dress to the register.

The attendant from earlier was there, and our eyes met.

Please don't give me that "Oh, so you're buying it for her? Good boy" look!

I paid for it and gave Fushimi the bag. "Have this as a souvenir from today."

"A-a souvenir of our first date…"

Hey, I didn't say that.

Is that really how she saw today…?

Fushimi started overheating again as she hugged the bag to her chest. "Thanks, Ryou."

I couldn't look straight at her, so I turned around and muttered, "S-sure."

Fushimi was in high spirits as she and I wandered about the mall.

Before we realized it, it was dark outside—it felt safe to say it was already night.

"Oh, it's almost six o'clock."

"Time flies, eh?"

She hadn't told me she had a curfew or anything, but I figured it wouldn't be good to stay out too late.

"Shall we go home?"

The joy left Fushimi's expression the moment she heard me say that. "…Yeah. We should."

"I'd never gone out like this before. It was fun."

"I—I had fun, too!"

When we'd hung out before, it'd always been in a more childish way: playing at the park or doing something at home—as if we were still in elementary school. This was the first time we passed the time like normal high schoolers.

"There's one last place I want to go," Fushimi said as we were heading for the exit. "I heard there's a pretty garden on the rooftop that gets lit up at night."

She wanted to see it, so we made our way there.

We found the garden as soon as we stepped off the elevator. There were flowers and other seasonal plants, plus an artificial streamlet.

"It's so pretty."

The lighting was carefully placed to illuminate the leaves and flowers.

"It is," I replied while we walked through the garden.

But the streamlet's running water wasn't the only sound I could hear—there was something smacking.

What's that?

I soon found the source of the mysterious noise: a couple sitting on a bench, cuddling and smooching.

"!"

R-right here?! In public?! I get this is a romantic spot, but man.

I turned back to Fushimi, and she was frozen in place.

"..."

The sight of the couple was too graphic for us inexperienced kids.

"Oh no. No further."

"C'mon—nobody's watching."

The shock was like walking into the adult corner of a video shop for the first time when you're too young for it. Like having your world forcefully expanded in a way you didn't expect.

"F-Fushimi, l-let's go..."

Her brain had completely stopped, so I pulled her hand and led us through the garden.

However...most of the benches were occupied by couples. Talk about a steamy situation.

"I don't think we b-belong here..."

"Y-y-yeah..."

We hastily made our way out of there, staring at our feet.

"...Why? They're outside... The garden was so pretty... Th-they shouldn't be doing that there." Fushimi was almost crying.

For her, that was probably like clicking a cat video only to be greeted with gore. I sympathized.

"And I thought this would be a great way to end our date..."

"The garden itself was pretty, so it's fine."

"If you say so…"

But yeah, they seemed ready to jump each other right there and then…

We were still too pure for the make-out garden, so we fled like low-level adventurers retreating from a high-level dungeon.

"Ouch…" Fushimi crouched down.

"What's wrong?"

"Nothing, I'm fine. It's just that my shoe slipped off a bit…"

I took a look, and some of the skin on her heel had been scraped off, enough to make me feel the pain, too.

…

Oh. So that's what it's for.

"Here, I have a Band-Aid. Take it."

"Are you sure?"

"Yeah. This is probably *why* I have it."

"?"

That damn gyaru is too smart.

Fushimi sat down on a bench right next to a vending machine, then put her leg up.

Wait a second, Fushimi—they're going public…

"W-wait. I'll put it on for you."

"What?! N-no, I'm fine."

"I can't let you do it like that. C'mon—put your foot over here."

"I-I've been walking all day long—I—I—I—I—I can't let you!"

"But your panties are showing!"

"Bw-w-w-uh?! Don't look!" Fushimi closed her legs in a panic and pulled her hem down.

"It's not like I did it on purpose. They just appeared…"

"Grrr…" Fushimi growled like a dog on guard, then gave me the Band-Aid and plopped her foot on my knee.

"D-don't sniff it, okay…?"

"Why would I do that, you idiot?! I'm not a degenerate."

"Hold your breath, just in case."

"So you're just that sure you have smelly feet?"

"Godddd, stop iiiiit!"

"Hey! Hold on! Don't kick—I'll…"

Too late— I saw her panties again…

I wrestled her leg and put the Band-Aid on.

There we go.

"You're so mean." She puffed her cheeks.

"You're the crazy person making me hold my breath…" I couldn't contain my laughter.

"And now you're laughing…"

"Sorry, sorry." I apologized again and again, but she didn't forgive me.

While we were on our way back to the station, Fushimi said, "Thanks for the Band-Aid. It really worked."

"Ah, Mana's the one who gave me that, so thank her."

She giggled. "You could've kept your secret and taken credit for being so considerate and reliable. You're so honest."

"I don't need a reputation for being considerate."

"And I don't think I'm as good or honest as you think, Ryou."

"Maybe not by your standards, but by mine, I'm pretty sure you are."

"Not at all," she said.

It was almost eight PM by the time we got to the station closest to our houses.

"Sorry we stayed out so late," I said.

"No, I was the one who said I wanted to go somewhere else first."

Even though the road was the same one we took from school every day, walking down it at night had a totally different feel.

Both the townscape and Fushimi by my side felt as if they were from a parallel world.

"Ryou, do you have more Band-Aids?"

"Did it slip off? Sorry, I only had the one."

"I see. Oh well, we're almost there."

We should've gone on bike. But the parking fee was too much for my poor high-schooler wallet.

She started walking more slowly, as if she was hurting.

"…"

I looked around to confirm no one was watching—not that anyone would recognize us in the middle of the night—and I crouched down in front of Fushimi.

"Here, get on."

"Huh? N-no, I'm too heavy."

"It'll be faster like this. And it hurts, right?"

"…Okay… If you say so." She put her arms around my neck and clung to my back.

…Not that I was expecting anything else, but I really couldn't feel anything from her chest area.

I made no comment about it, since that would give her free rein to bash my head from above.

"Am I heavy?"

"You are not."

Her arms around my neck tightened, and she whispered into my ear, "…Thanks."

"You're welcome."

With Fushimi on my back, I walked down the street among the glow of the streetlights.

◆**Shizuka Torigoe**◆

I was playing games on my phone Saturday night, when I received a couple of texts.

Ping! A third one arrived. I opened them up.

From Hina:

It went well today!

Not perfectly, but ^^;

I never would've done it if you hadn't encouraged me to ask him! Thank you!

Guess Fushimi had fun on her date with Takamori—she even messaged me about it.

So sincere and polite.

I still wasn't quite sure how to interact with her. Takamori's rapport with her I could understand, what with them being childhood friends, but I didn't have that connection.

Eventually, I just replied, You're welcome.

Talking with the princess of the school always made me feel inferior, and I wanted to distance myself from her. You could probably see it in that short, straightforward response.

She's a good person, I know, but...

As the saying goes, no fish will live in water too clean, and the Fushimi River is too pure for me.

Approaching her was especially hard considering I was the plain librarian no one paid attention to.

Meanwhile, Fushimi's followers were there by her side during every single break.

I don't know what Takamori thinks, but to me, it seems many of her followers are just trying to get a leg up in the social hierarchy.

It was too obvious they were trying to use that Fushimi buff I'd talked to Takamori about, and I didn't like anybody whose only interest was pretending they were interesting.

Wanna eat lunch together sometime?

When Fushimi texted me, I thought for a while about how to reply. If she went to the physics room, her hangers-on would follow, as they did.

"I...wouldn't like that, no...," I muttered to my phone while lying on my bed. It was pretty obvious it wasn't *me* she wanted to have lunch with.

If I accept, then she'll easily have access to the physics room, where Takamori also spends lunchtime.

Although...I wonder. Is that really it?

She didn't seem like the type to hide her true intentions, so maybe she really just wanted to have lunch with me.

"...In any case..."

Hina Fushimi was at the center of our class—of our whole school, really. She would attract all the iron sand like the magnet she was, bringing that unwanted company with her.

It wasn't Fushimi's fault, although, I did wish she were more aware of her own position. Maybe that was her only failing.

Even so, I couldn't turn her down. A pleb like me didn't have the right to turn down the princess.

That was how school society worked.

I sent another blunt reply.

◆Hina Fushimi◆

Once I finished basking in the afterglow of my date with Ryou, I sent Torigoe a message thanking her and asking her to have lunch together.

OK

The reply took a while to arrive.

"Oh, good…"

I was getting worried she actually hated me. After all, I'd taken the title of class rep from her.

The reply was pretty blunt, but that was how she seemed to be. The kind of girl who's probably always quiet, reading some book while holding her head in her hand.

Every time I asked her what she always talked about with Ryou during lunchtime, she never gave me much of a reply: "Nothing." "Not much." And so on.

Even if they didn't talk, they must spend lunch together because they find each other's presence comfortable.

I was curious to know what kind of girl would make Ryou feel like that, and I hoped to make her a friend.

"It's a quiet place…so I wouldn't want everyone making it all noisy…"

I mulled it over, trying to find a way to be alone during lunch. I didn't want to ruin their break.

Ryouuuuu

I texted him, and he immediately answered:

?

Knowing the guy I loved would answer when I called gave me a thrill of joy.

Can I visit you at the physics room during lunch?

no

That was fast… Now I'm sad…

But I'd expected that answer.

Even if he wasn't the greatest at reading the room or whatever, he never beat around the bush. It felt good just seeing him. He never wore a mask, whether it was with me or with our classmates or even with our teachers. He never pretended to be someone else.

Meanwhile, everyone else—and I mean literally *everyone* else—always paid attention to the time, place, and occasion; they always tried to see where the wind was blowing; they always concerned themselves with what others would think—they always pretended to be someone else.

Ryou could be himself at school, and that made him a hero in my eyes.

He never forced himself to do anything he didn't want, no matter who he was talking to, and that gave me this special sense of calm.

Although he also never holds back, so sometimes his remarks can cut pretty deep...

I found it strange when I started talking to him again, since I didn't really remember that side of him. But it was refreshing and made me want to know him even more.

Despite our history together, we hadn't really had much contact since middle school. I only knew his grade-school self.

I never knew what he was like during that in-between period, and I was only now getting to know him as a high schooler. Of course, I knew what he was like in the classroom, but that's only, like, twenty percent of your true self.

I wrote and rewrote a new message for Torigoe again and again, but I didn't know what to say. I ended up closing the app.

...Maybe Torigoe was the one who knew Ryou better now. The idea made my chest hurt just a little bit.

Monday was here, and I languidly dragged myself to school alongside Fushimi.

I didn't know when we'd fallen back into our familiar friendship. Or maybe it was just me.

My status as the childhood friend who always accompanied Hina Fushimi (important: not boyfriend) had already spread throughout the entire school, and I was receiving fewer envious glares.

That day, as on any other day, I largely let the information from all my classes go in one ear and out the other, while also fulfilling my duties as class rep.

Another nothing kinda day, I thought right before lunchtime.

Someone knocked on the door of the physics room.

I turned to look at Torigoe across the room, and we both tilted our heads.

"If you'll excuse me!" The door opened, letting Fushimi in.

"...What're you doing here?"

"C'mon, Ryou—that's no way to greet a friend. I just came here because I promised Torigoe I'd have lunch with her."

She stuck her tongue out and walked over to Torigoe.

I worried her followers would be here, too, but there was no sign of them.

"What about everyone else?" I asked.

"Ah... Ha-ha. I said I'd go to the restroom to get them off my tail."

Good call—otherwise they'd be here, too.

"Poor guys," I joked. I had no sympathy for them in the slightest.

"What else am I supposed to do? I want to spend the break in peace, too."

I didn't even have to see her to know she was puffing out her cheeks.

Promised to have lunch with her...? What are you, a grade-schooler?

I could hear their conversation while I made steady progress on the lunch Mana had prepared for me.

Isn't this the first time they've talked face-to-face? As far as I know, at least.

Fushimi had come well prepared for her meeting—she talked about things Torigoe would find interesting, which were mostly novels.

This is the first time I'm hearing Fushimi talk about books.

She probably never brought up the topic with me because I wasn't much of a reader.

"The movie was so good I had to read the book, and once I got to the middle, I couldn't put it down!"

"Yeah. That author is pretty good at suspense. Even when it's scary, you get so invested you have to know what happens next."

"R-right? It wasn't like that in the movie... I stayed up until two in the morning because I had to finish it..."

"Same!"

They were having so much fun.

Fushimi could never talk so excitedly about books with her followers, so I imagined she felt some kind of special kinship with Torigoe.

...Have I ever had someone I could talk with like that...?

...Oh no. The first person who came to mind was Mana.

I thought Torigoe was similar to me in the few-friends department, but at least she could have fun talking to people about her hobbies...

It was kinda...depressing...

They gave each other recommendations to keep the fun going.

I see. So she agreed to have lunch with Torigoe because she wanted to talk about novels.

This wasn't her princess facade—it was much closer to her true face than what she showed in the classroom.

I'd been thinking she'd have a much easier time if she just acted like that with people other than me, but now that it was happening, I felt a little left out.

Not that I want to keep the real Fushimi all to myself. She needs friends.

I'd finished my lunch and started playing games on my phone for lack of anything better to do, when I heard people approaching in the hallways.

I checked the clock, and there were still twenty minutes left until fifth period started.

Right away, I recognized the voices.

The door opened loudly, revealing three girls and two boys.

"Hina, we looked everywhere for you!"

"What are you doing *here?*"

Fushimi's hangers-on had arrived. They must've gotten tired of waiting for her.

A cloud crossed Fushimi's face for just a second before turning into the elegant smile she always showed in the classroom.

"Sorry. I remembered I had something to do while I was in the bathroom."

They formed a circle around her like always, not even giving Torigoe the time of day.

"What were you talking about with Torigoe?"

"This place is really quiet, huh? It's nice."

"The cafeteria is always so noisy. We should come here all the time instead, too."

"Huh? But then…" Fushimi panicked.

Torigoe silently grabbed her stuff and left the room, while Fushimi seemed troubled, shocked, and full of regret.

I winked at Fushimi and stood up. *I'll handle her.*

I didn't know if she got what I was getting at, but she moved her head slightly. I was gonna take that as a nod.

Their voices echoed loudly throughout the quiet physics room.

I wandered around the school, searching for Torigoe, until I found her at the library's counter, reading a book.

I grabbed a book from the shelves and put it on the counter. "...Is this what you recommended to Fushimi just now?"

"Hey, Takamori."

I leaned on the counter, supporting myself with my hand behind my back. "This stuff's complicated," I said. "It's not like they did anything bad."

"Yeah. You're right. I do wish they'd pay attention to how the rest of us feel, but they always act like that, even in the classroom."

"Plus, we're using the physics room without anyone's permission. They should be free to use it, too."

"Yeah," she agreed.

That was the kind of people they were, and this was the kind of people we were. It was like a jigsaw puzzle. No single piece is good or bad—they only either fit or don't.

"I kinda saw it coming when Fushimi asked me to let her join for lunch." The novel I was borrowing was placed next to my hand. "You have two weeks. May third will be during the Golden Week holidays, so please return it on the sixth," she told me in a near monotone.

"You should've turned her down if you didn't want her coming."

"The only one brave enough to do that in the hierarchy we live in is you, Takamori."

"Hierarchy...? Don't be so dramatic."

I knew Fushimi cared about that sort of thing, but it was a bit surprising to find out Torigoe did, too.

"Even if you did turn her down, Fushimi wouldn't go talking behind your back."

"I know. She abandoned her followers to come be with us because she knew we wouldn't get along with them."

"That's the kind of person she is. She may be stubborn and uptight at times, but she's a master at reading the room. Please cut her some slack this time."

I heard Torigoe snort behind my back. "I'm not mad—don't worry. This always happens."

People like us only wanted to spend time in peace and quiet, but we always ended up being driven away.

"Yeah, it's just... You know. I don't want you to rethink it after this and stop talking about books with her."

"Takamori, what are you to her?" There was a slight laugh in her voice.

"I'm her childhood friend."

"Well, childhood friends don't usually worry that much about each other."

Really? I tilted my head.

"When you get along really, really well and end up feeling like family, I don't think you usually notice those kinds of things."

...True, maybe I wouldn't have worried that much if "childhood friend" was the only label for our relationship.

Back then, I saw her as the popular girl who could get along with anyone, so I would've just concluded she'd be able to take care of it by herself.

"Damn...," Torigoe muttered. "She's more friendly than I thought. She's cute and kind and can keep up with my conversations about books... Dammit..."

Apparently, Fushimi far exceeded what Torigoe had expected out of her.

I turned my head around, and Torigoe immediately returned her focus to her librarian work.

"...Torigoe, there's only five minutes left until the break ends, you know that?"

"I know."

She gathered a few books to her chest to return them to the bookshelves. I volunteered to help her out.

I placed the books in alphabetical order by author, just as she said. We were standing back-to-back, placing books on opposite shelves, when she suddenly spoke up with some tension in her voice.

"T-Takamori…is there anyone you like?"

"What—?"

The question caught me off guard.

"Is there anyone you like?"

I turned around only to find Torigoe nonchalantly doing her job, sliding another book into place.

"…That baseball player. The legend. I like him," I said.

"Who, Nomo?"

"Really? You think that's who I meant?"

"…Could ask you the same thing," she muttered, urging me to answer seriously. "Hurry up, or class is gonna start without its class rep."

"Well, excuse me for being slow. I'm not used to this job."

But it was kinda brazen of me to complain after volunteering to help her. I handed her the few books I had left, and she swiftly put them on the shelves.

"Now we're done. Thanks."

"No need to thank me. Not like I was much help, anyway."

She shook her head, and her silky hair swayed. "For the thought, not for any actual help."

"O-oh… Okay, then…," I answered faintly before leaving the library.

Back at the classroom, Fushimi gave me a worried look.

The teacher came, we did the greetings, and once class began, we started writing back and forth.

Was Torigoe okay?

She's fine. She understands it's no one's fault.

From what I could tell, Fushimi didn't have any real, true friends, despite having an excess of people to talk to. I wanted her to get along with Torigoe. I knew them both individually, and I was very surprised to see them chatting so freely. I never would have guessed they'd be friends.

Sorry. I won't go to the physics room anymore.

As soon as I finished reading that, I raised my head to see that she was forcing a smile.

Torigoe would appreciate that; it was her time and place to be in peace and quiet, free from worrying about anyone else.

That was when I realized. They didn't have to limit themselves to lunchtime to get along.

Wanna go somewhere with Torigoe after school?

She nodded.

Now I have to get the other one to accept.

Fushimi started sneakily tapping at her phone below her desk, keeping her eyes on the blackboard.

We couldn't look at Torigoe, since she was behind us.

After what seemed like a few messages, Fushimi made a circle with her fingers to signal Torigoe had given us the okay.

I'm glad Torigoe still wants to be friends with her.

Classes ended, and Fushimi wrote in the class journal while Torigoe stayed at her seat, glued to her phone.

"What're you looking at?"

"Manga."

A fan of the digital versions, eh?

"All done!" Fushimi closed the journal with a thud, grabbed her bag, and stood up. We did the same.

"Fushimi, are you sure?" Torigoe asked.

"Yes. I wouldn't ask you otherwise."

"No... I don't mean it in that way..." Torigoe scratched her cheek, troubled.

I couldn't tell what she meant, and apparently Fushimi couldn't, either, as she turned to look at me.

We left the classroom and went to the staff room to deliver the journal, then headed out.

"Ryou, any idea where we should go?"

"How about the library? Not the school's, obviously—a city library. There's a big one pretty close to here."

One time, I left school early and spent a few hours there until it was time for my mom to leave for work. Couldn't go straight home and have her finding out I faked being sick.

"What do you think, Torigoe?"

"Sounds good."

And so our destination was decided.

Torigoe didn't seem to be upset at Fushimi, maybe thanks to our talk back during lunchtime. The wall between them wasn't totally gone, either, but I could see some progress.

It took us just barely over five minutes to get to the city library on foot.

"I-it's huge…" Torigoe sounded surprised.

"It's as big as a gymnasium." Fushimi's comparison was on point.

There were bookshelves everywhere, and that special smell of carpet and old books filled the air.

"This place is perfect for us, but what're you going to do here, Ryou?"

Fushimi seemed to think I'd never held a book in my life. And yeah, I wouldn't call myself an avid reader. Obviously, the possibility of me doing homework instead would never have crossed her mind.

"What do you mean, what am I going to do? Well, of course, silently read a book by the window."

"Ha-ha-ha."

"Hey, don't laugh. I wasn't joking."

I took the book I borrowed during lunch out from my bag.

"Ah… That."

"It's the one Torigoe recommended. I'll be reading it. By the window."

"What's the deal with the window?" Fushimi asked, and Torigoe giggled.

I'll leave the bookworms all alone to bookworm it up.

I headed for the reading space so as to not bother them.

There were a few people already there studying, probably third-years preparing for entrance exams. I gave them their space, too, and sat right by the window, just as I'd said I would.

Once I saw the other two disappear into the sea of bookshelves, I opened my book.

I bet they'll be friends in no time.

◆**Shizuka Torigoe**◆

"This one's great!"

Fushimi's taste in books was quite refined. She had read authors I'd never heard of, and she had already gone through the works of others I was interested in.

There were few books we had both read, but all the ones she had under her belt were incredibly interesting. I was having a great time asking her about all of them.

"This one's kinda moody. You feel like it's raining all the time while reading it."

"You...really love tragedies, don't you?"

"Ah... Yeah, I guess you could say that."

A lot of the books she recommended had tragic endings or were about the protagonist going through some sort of hell. I would've pegged her as more of a fan of fluffy, girly stories, so the revelation came as quite a surprise.

"Wow."

"Is it that shocking?"

That dissonance worked in her favor to make her more interesting.

Honestly, I envied her. Fushimi would get points for being intellectual with a book in her hand, while the same behavior on me just added to my gloomy vibe.

"...Why did you invite me? I'm only getting in the way."

I knew they always went back home together, just the two of them.

"Ryou was the one who suggested it. And I also wanted to get along with you."

"...I see."

What...is he thinking?

I looked around for him and found him at the reading space—right by the window, just as he'd said, with the hardcover book open in front of him.

He had his head resting on his hand...and was fast asleep. He would.

I had to smile. "After all that insisting that he'd be reading, now he's sleeping."

Fushimi noticed it, too, and laughed.

""Right by the window!"" we said at the same time, then let out muffled giggles.

I felt the same thing I had back during lunch—I didn't like the princess act when everyone else was around, but once I saw her laugh like this, I couldn't bring myself to hate her.

For that same reason, I wanted to ask her. I wanted to tell her.

These few seconds of laughter made up my mind.

"Fushimi, what would you do if you met a girl who liked Takamori?"

"What...? Why the sudden question?"

She must've realized—her cute face turned grim. She tried to hide it behind a smile, but it was obviously artificial.

"'Cause I think *I*...like...Takamori."

There was a drizzle outside, light enough to not need an umbrella.

The clock on the wall showed it was almost five PM.

The novel Torigoe had recommended was still open on the table. I had no memory of anything past the first three pages I'd skimmed.

"Oh, you're up."

Fushimi was sitting in front of me. She had a paperback in one hand, her head resting on the other as she looked at me.

"Guess the silence here is perfect for napping, huh?"

"We're not allowed to talk in here," I retorted jokingly.

"No one will care as long as we keep our voices down." Fushimi seemed offended. There was no one around, so she was right that there would be no problem.

"Where's Torigoe?" I asked.

"...She left. I guess she didn't find anything interesting."

"Oh. I see. So are you friends now?"

She awkwardly laughed as she glanced at the entrance. "We do seem to have similar taste."

Figures. That's why I chose the library.

"Yeah, it's easier to really get into a conversation about something you have in common."

"No... Well, yeah. In a sense." She frowned, then forced a smile. "I guess I could see our talks getting quite heated."

"Huh. Does she think the same?"

Everyone gets heated when it comes to the things they like, at least in my opinion.

"Yeah."

I could feel something hidden behind her smile. What had happened?

They seemed to have so much in common... Or maybe they had different points of view on the same hobby, and maybe they'd gotten in an argument. Like they could've been sharing their views and realized they disagreed.

But you can't even get to that point if you don't have the same passion for your hobby.

"I'm glad you have someone to chat with, even if you end up disagreeing."

"Yeah...," she replied languidly.

Now that Torigoe was gone, we had no reason to stay at the library. We headed to the train station through the sprinkling drizzle.

◆Hina Fushimi◆

"See you."

Ryou said good-bye at my doorstep, and I watched him go back home.

The drizzle had already stopped by the time we reached the station nearest to our neighborhood, leaving behind only that peculiar dusty smell that comes after rain.

Ryou turned around and shooed me away with his hand, telling me not to stay all night there watching him and that I should go inside already.

I waved at him, happy that he turned to look at me again. He shrugged and continued on his way home. I watched him until I could no longer see his back.

"I think I...like...Takamori."

I still couldn't get those words out of my mind.

I hadn't been able to say anything back; I'd just frozen there in between the bookshelves. Torigoe had told me to my face she liked my childhood friend.

I entered my empty home and collapsed into my bed.

"You didn't have to...be so nice about telling me..."

I had never directly touched the topic with Ryou. I'd never asked him who he liked, nor had he told me about any crushes he might have.

I had never even heard any rumors about it. If it had ever come up, I was sure one of the nosy, gossipy girls would've mentioned it.

Because of that, I had always felt safe in the knowledge that no one would take him from me.

"Hmm... I was too conceited... Typical childhood-friend arrogance."

I'd thought wrong. But I wasn't being neglectful, either. I had told him. Many times. And he hadn't noticed.

"Ryou, you stupid idiot."

It must be because he likes bigger boobs...

The porn DVDs he'd had in his room when I visited the other day were all like that.

And I was still developing.

I'd taken a peek during PE, and Torigoe's breasts...weren't big. At all.

But they were bigger than mine!

"...It hurts..."

I wonder what Ryou would think if Torigoe told him about her feelings.

She was the classmate he always spent lunch with, so it was certainly within the realm of possibility that she would. In fact, wasn't she the obvious choice?

"Ow... I'm getting anxious just thinking about it."

I was sweating, and the beating of my heart was unsteady. I was having trouble breathing.

My chest was aching as I pictured it.

I had only stepped in there today, but the physics room remained a special place for those two.

I was still interested in Torigoe—I still wanted to be friends with her, but...

"Telling me she likes Ryou is basically a declaration of war…"

After opening up at least a little to her, I thought we could be friends, but did this mean it was impossible after all? I mean, it was hard to be friends after a declaration of war. She'd proclaimed me as her enemy (in love, anyway).

It was shocking to think she felt that way when I just wanted to get along with her.

"I should've told him I like him on our date the other day! That's what I get for thinking he'd misunderstand again! My punishment for thinking I still had plenty of time!"

There was no time! I was so full of myself! This is why they say never to let your guard down.

And my guard was way too low.

I might've been closest to Ryou among the people he'd known since kindergarten, but I probably wasn't his number one overall.

Back when we were in grade school, I'd found a note in Ryou's notebook that got me so upset I tore it to pieces. It was my little sin, brought upon me by young love.

I still had the pieces in my desk drawer because I couldn't bring myself to throw them away. I couldn't just break people's things and then put them in the trash. I'd believed that if I kept it, it could still be put back together with tape and maybe lighten my karmic sentence. I'd locked it up in there.

I got my key and opened the small drawer, taking out the paper pieces.

Maybe he doesn't remember our promises because he doesn't think anything of me…

The scraps had Ryou's handwriting, saying, I like…, followed by the name of a girl who wasn't me.

Fushimi had been gloomy for the past few days, ever since we went to the library.

"Hey, Fushimi, we gotta do the greetings."

"Ah."

I had to remind her to do her job of class rep, which was a real role reversal. Everyone followed Fushimi's lead greeting the teacher, and class began.

Her expression would shift from spacey to serious to sometimes even sad. I asked what all that was about, but she only ever said, "It's nothing."

If it was truly nothing, you'd be acting like normal.

What if whatever was bothering her wasn't something a guy would understand?

Maybe I should get Mana to talk with her.

"For this next problem...Fushimi, can you show us how to solve it?"

"Huh? Ah, um..."

Her eyes were going from her textbook to the blackboard and back. She hadn't been paying attention.

"R-Ryou...do you know?" She begged me for help.

I smiled.

Sorry, Fushimi. I wasn't paying attention, either.

Good luck, I wrote in English.

"Why in English?"

"Were you not listening, Fushimi? Please pay more attention in class."

"Ack... Y-yes... I'm sorry..."

Now that you don't see every day.

Had something happened with her followers? Like…

"Let's go to the physics room for lunch from now on!"

"W-wait, no… Let's not go there again."

"No way! Why?"

Or something. Maybe they'd gotten in an argument?

In her attempts to protect the original inhabitants of the physics room, maybe she'd ended up upsetting them.

Yeah, I can see that happening.

Fushimi still seemed absentminded when break time started, so I tried to get her attention. "It's fine if they want to use the physics room, you know. Torigoe and I will look for another place."

"Torigoe and you…" Her eyes seemed almost wounded as she stared at me, slightly pouting, her eyebrows upturned. "……Oh… Okay…"

What is it? You want to say something, don't you?

"If there's anything you need to get off your chest, I'm happy to listen."

She glared at me with suspicion. "See, Ryou, that's the problem. I *have* said it. All of it. I've been saying it all this time! But you—! You just *neeeever* listen!" She started hitting me.

"Wait! Wait! What's wrong with you, Hina? Calm down!"

Everyone was staring at us, wondering why the princess was acting like a pouty little kid.

You're ruining your entire image, so stop hitting me! Or at least turn off your hamster face.

"Are you drunk or something?"

"I would be if I could!"

She's maxed out her sulkiness level…

She buried her puffy face in her desk. Without raising her head, she asked, "Hey, Ryou. Where are you having lunch today?"

"At the physics room, same as always."

"…Do you like Torigoe?"

"How did you get all the way there? Tell me, would you fall in love with someone just because you're in the same classroom as them?"

"That wouldn't be enough, but…"

I would've understood if we always had lunch sitting close together. It would've been easy to misinterpret our relationship that way. But we didn't. We sat around three desks apart from each other. We sometimes talked, but we weren't so close that things would be awkward if we weren't having a conversation.

"Ryou, you dense… You *can* read a room and then ignore it, and yet you don't get this… God, agh…"

"What're you going on about…?"

Fushimi is super tetchy today.

"Want a candy?"

"Ryou…you can't bring candy to school, you know?"

"C'mon—it's the fruit kind. Which one do you want?"

"Grape."

I knew that warning was just to keep up appearances—she still wanted it.

I took the candies out of my bag, placed the one Fushimi had requested on her desk, and picked out a lemon one for myself.

Fushimi grabbed hers. "It's good."

"I know, right?"

"You better eat them all before break ends."

"Yeah, yeah." I popped candy after candy into my mouth.

"Ryou, do you like large breasts?"

"Blugh?!" I almost spat out everything. "Where's that coming from…?"

"Do you not like them small?"

"I don't dislike them."

"R-really?"

Huh? Did her voice just suddenly get cheerier?

"I like all shapes and sizes."

"So you're saying you don't care whose they are?"

Uhhh? I mean, I guess...? But why are you staring at me like that? I'm pretty sure most guys feel this way...

The other classes went by until lunchtime came.

"Takamori, let's go."

"Huh?"

Torigoe came to my seat. She'd never done that during first year.

We weren't exactly having lunch *together*, so I didn't feel the need to invite her.

I guess if we're in the same class, and we're both going to the physics room, it wouldn't be weird for us to walk there together...?

"Ah, yeah..."

I was a bit puzzled internally, but I gathered my stuff and stood up. Fushimi was watching me with abandoned-puppy eyes.

"..."

She looked as if she wanted to say something but couldn't.

Torigoe glanced at her, and their eyes met.

Fushimi shook her head, slapped her cheeks, and stood up. "Sorry, guys. I'm having lunch with Ryou and Torigoe today."

Her eyes had suddenly blazed up with fighting spirit for...some reason. The energy was so intense that it apparently even kept her followers from coming after us.

"Ryou, let's go."

"W-wait..."

She grabbed my hand and stomped her way out of the classroom, pulling me with her.

Torigoe followed, walking gracefully beside her.

"I won't hesitate anymore," Fushimi said.

"Heh. I see."

Wh-what's up with you two? Didn't you become friends just the other day?

They sure didn't feel like friends anymore. That much I could tell. But...what was going on...?

We entered the physics room, and I sat at my usual spot. Fushimi took the seat right next to me.

"So you've got the *gyaru* lunch for today, eh, Ryou?"

"Yeah. Mana's been making my lunch lately."

She'd stop whenever I skipped class or got bad marks on my tests. She was more like my mother than my sister—although all of this was under my actual mom's direct orders.

Torigoe walked all the way to us, then took the spot in front of me.

"...Is this seat free?"

"Yeah, as you can see."

Torigoe opened her lunch box in silence, while Fushimi also quietly started eating hers.

...What's up with these two today? Is it like National Falling-Out Day or something?

"So you're not sitting in your usual place, Torigoe?"

"Nope," she replied bluntly, then put another bite in her mouth.

"Fushimi...are you sure you won't have any problems leaving the others?"

"This is an emergency, so yes."

"O-okay..."

An emergency for me, maybe.

They weren't speaking at all—the silence was taxing.

I tried various topics they'd probably like, but neither of them reacted as I'd hoped.

"...Are you two mad at each other?"

That was the only possible conclusion. A wise man once said, "Only true friends get truly mad at each other."

"It'd be easier if we were," Fushimi said with a sigh.

"It's not as simple as that, Takamori."

It's not?

"Then what is it? Tell me, please."

I looked at Fushimi, to no avail. Then I turned to Torigoe, and she put her chopsticks down.

"Takamori, there's something I want to tell you after school."

Fushimi's shoulders jumped; she was shaking as her head swiveled back and forth between me and Torigoe.

"After school? Okay."

"I'll see you in the classroom."

"You could tell me now."

"I can't tell you now. That's why I said that."

"...I guess."

I didn't object, but what could it be that she couldn't tell me right then?

Torigoe sighed, rested her head on her hand, and looked at Fushimi and me. "You and Fushimi go way back, right?"

Fushimi nodded before I could answer. "Yeah. We stopped talking for a while, but we've been friends ever since grade school. A-and even now... we're still..." Her voice turned quieter and quieter as she replied.

Torigoe snorted. It felt vaguely aggressive, almost as if she was trying to rile Fushimi. It was strange. Was Torigoe always this kind of person?

"Do you know why the girl who's always been by the protagonist's side always loses out in manga, anime, movies, and everything else?"

"It happens to guys, too. The first boy who likes the protagonist of a girls' manga never ends up winning."

"Yup. And the reason for that is that they're never exciting enough."

Fushimi said nothing, which was a silent acknowledgment of that point.

"Since they've known their friend for such a long time, they've already experienced most things with them. It's not enough to truly get their heart pumping."

Fushimi cast her eyes down. She'd been trying to object to everything Torigoe was saying, but that flame of defiance was quickly being extinguished.

"You've been with them forever, so you don't really care about knowing them further. On the other hand, if you're interested in someone new, you'll be more invested in the process."

"...!" Fushimi quietly gasped.

There was something going on behind this conversation, but I didn't get any of it except that Torigoe was somehow tormenting Fushimi.

"Torigoe, let's stop this. I don't get where the conversation is going."

"I'm not talking to you, Takamori."

"And that's why I'm telling you to stop."

"Sorry... I just remembered I've got some class-rep stuff to do." Fushimi stood up with a thud and left the physics room.

Torigoe let out a long sigh after she was gone. "Geez..."

It was hard to understand what Torigoe was thinking, since she never really talked, but now that she *was* talking, she was even more incomprehensible.

"...Wait for me after school, okay?"

"Yeah, yeah."

"You don't have rep stuff to take care of?"

"...There's nothing we have to do during lunch."

Maybe checking where the next class would be and doing preparations, but nothing else. The next class that day was classical literature, which was always held at our classroom. There were no materials to prepare.

"I know I'm right, but I might've been too harsh...," Torigoe muttered and frowned.

"Is there really any need to 'truly get your heart pumping'? I don't believe there is."

"Then you should've said so."

"Why?"

We are *talking about manga, right?*

Right then, I had a revelation. "Oh, are you fighting because you like different characters in a manga?!"

"No."

Damn, and I was sure I had it.

"Seriously, why the hell would you...? No, that's not it. At all."

"Don't deny it twice!"

Why do you sound so fed up?

Once Fushimi was gone, Torigoe returned to her usual place, and we spent the rest of lunchtime in silence.

The last periods of the school day came and went. It was Fushimi's turn to write in the class journal, but she left as soon as the last class ended.

There was no rule saying the journal should be written inside the classroom, so I assumed she'd do it somewhere else.

Usually, though, she'd write it while chatting in here. Maybe it had something to do with Torigoe wanting to talk with me?

I turned around to find Torigoe tapping at her phone; maybe she didn't want to talk right away.

People who had club activities left the classroom right away, while the others discussed where to go hang out before leaving. All the other conversations disappeared after around ten minutes, leaving only Torigoe and me there.

I sat backward in my chair, leaning my chest against the backrest.

"So what did you want to tell me?" I asked.

Torigoe put her phone down. "You haven't noticed, but your stock has been going up lately."

"...Are we talking about finance or something?"

"Your social stock."

Social stock? "Oh, that Fushimi-buff thing you were talking about?"

"There's also that, but remember when you told off Matsuzaka's crew for talking behind her back?"

Oh, that thing about her helping out at the tennis tournament?

"Apparently, a lot of the girls fell for you after that."

"And how can you know that?"

"There's this thing called 'group chats'—ever heard of it?"

"You think I'm dumb or something?" *I just wasn't invited—doesn't mean I don't know the concept.*

"Well, it came up in there, and everyone started liking you more."

"Huh. I thought they'd start hating me. Everything was extremely awkward after that."

"These are two very different things."

Is that how girls work?

"Up until this April, I thought I was the only one you got along with."

And you wouldn't be wrong.

I never spoke to anyone in class, while I did chat a bit with my physics-room lunchmate.

"And when I found out you were Fushimi's childhood friend...I started worrying that maybe I wasn't your number one... So... Um...," she stammered as she looked for the right words. "It kinda stung."

She looked as if she had something more to say, so I waited for her to continue.

"I wondered why. It didn't really make sense why I'd be sad."

She'd thought she was my best friend, but it turned out that wasn't the case.

I had experienced that several times during grade school. It did sting, thinking you were someone's best friend and then finding out they liked someone else more. Made you feel lonely.

"But I didn't just feel sad, actually. It was something else, not what

©Fly

you'd have for a friend—it was more…romantic." Torigoe groaned quietly and looked down. "…I didn't like that you got along with Fushimi. I hated it—*hated* that a girl like her was in the picture. I didn't stand a chance."

How would I have felt in her place? Would I have hated it if I saw Torigoe getting along with another boy once we got to second year?

If anything, I probably would've been relieved. I would've been glad that she had someone else to talk to.

"So when I thought about why I didn't like it, there was only one answer…"

"Yeah?"

"I finally realized. I'm in love with you, Takamori."

"…Takamori?"

"Me?"

"Yes."

…I knew Torigoe wasn't the type to joke around about this subject.

"M-me?"

"…Yes."

Now I'm confused.

I had never seen her in that way before. "Um, okay…"

"Yeah."

Wh-what do you say in times like this? I was too panicked to think about what to say.

"Please don't look so confused." She smiled kindly, if awkwardly.

"S-sorry. I didn't think that was where this was going."

"I'm pretty sure anyone could guess exactly where this was going as soon as a girl says she wants to talk to youafter school."

Sh-she's right… She's totally right, but I wasn't expecting it.

"G-give me a sec," I begged.

"Sure. Take however long you need," she replied, staring at me.

Torigoe certainly is quite pretty. She's quiet and a bit aloof, which makes some people think she's boring, but that's not the case, and I know it.

I bet we'd have a great time together if we did go out. It'd be comfy, like our time in the physics room. We can understand each other without saying too much—silence wouldn't be a negative in our relationship.

"..."

Then Fushimi's face crossed my mind.

I didn't understand why it was her, but there had to be a reason it wasn't Mana or any other girl.

The silence was broken with a clatter. I turned to the source and found the silhouette of a girl running in the hallway.

That's...

"God...," Torigoe whispered, then pointed outside. "Just run after her. It's probably Fushimi."

"Huh?"

"Go already!"

The way her voice suddenly rose stunned me for just an instant, then the distress in her words finally got through.

I hurried out of the classroom and into the hallway. I saw her black hair swaying as she ran, and I hurried after her per Torigoe's advice.

She was moving as fast as ever, faster than I'd ever be able to run—but I followed her anyway.

"Fushimi!"

Why had she been outside the classroom? Was she curious about what Torigoe would tell me?

"Wait!"

But what will I tell her once I catch up?

I might've had nothing to say, but I knew I had to catch her.

"...!"

I could tell she was crying, even from behind.

I chased her until we got all the way to the stairway leading to the rooftop. She was cornered now. The door to the rooftop was locked, so she had no escape.

"...I told you to wait... How long were you planning on running...?" I had been expecting this game of tag to end quickly, but it took, like, ten minutes. "I doubt you've ever tried going up to the roof, Miss Model

Student, but you can't go up there." It was all I could do just to catch my breath.

At the top of the stairs, she sniffled without turning around and feebly replied, "Why…did you follow me?"

"Because you ran away. After eavesdropping on us, too… Didn't anyone teach you not to do that?"

"I'm…sorry about that. I was listening and got curious and…ended up going all the way to the classroom…"

You were listening?

Fushimi wiped her eyes with her hands. "So what are you telling her?"

"……Ah, yeah…" I scratched my head. "I feel bad about it, but I'm gonna say no."

"Why?"

"I don't know."

"How can you not know…?"

"When I thought about what to answer, the first thing that came to mind was you." And I had no idea why. "I felt like…if I accepted, we'd go back to being just classmates."

"What's wrong with that? We've been classmates for years."

"There's a lot wrong with it." Even as I said the words, I didn't quite understand what they meant. I just knew I couldn't let her run away in tears. "I feel better with you next to me."

She sniffled again, and her shoulders trembled.

"Not anyone else. It has to be you."

Fushimi finally turned around to face me. Her face was a teary mess— the total opposite of the school's princess.

"Right back at you!"

She ran and leaped from the top of the stairs all the way to where I was standing.

She fell right into my arms, and I embraced her…then fell backward, hitting my head hard on the floor.

"O-ouch!"

"S-sorry… I couldn't contain myself." Fushimi was on top of me, her long eyelashes wet with tears and her eyes red.

"You look awful," I commented.

"And whose fault would that be?"

My phone chirped, and I took a look at the text that arrived. It was from Torigoe.

I'm going home. No need to answer back. I'm fine.

"Torigoe?"

"Ryou, truth be told…"

◆Shizuka Torigoe◆

I'm going home. No need to answer back. I'm fine.

Once I'd sent that message to Takamori, I buried my face in the desk.

"Those two are such a hassle…"

I was tired after dealing with Fushimi, who wasn't doing anything she was supposed to, and Takamori, who simply never got anything when it was about himself.

After school, I called Fushimi, then left my phone in my pocket while I talked to Takamori so that she would hear everything.

And the end result was that I'd been rejected.

I grabbed my bag, stood up, and left the school.

"I knew this would happen."

It was obvious that they were in love with each other—at least, to anyone paying attention. Many of the girls didn't see it.

I liked Takamori, but I'd also started liking Fushimi after talking with her.

So I had to warn her that another girl could take him from her. I'd declared war on her to light a fire under her butt and get them together already.

…It's for the best; Takamori should stay with someone as perfect as Fushimi. I wouldn't be okay losing to anyone else.

I'd played with their feelings for my own satisfaction, and I did want to apologize for that.

"But it's your own faults for being so wishy-washy."

I'd tried to make Takamori realize his feelings for Fushimi, but her getting impatient and showing up herself had not been in my plans.

"She couldn't wait for Takamori to come to a conclusion, I guess."

...And it was the same for me.

Day after day, seeing them having fun during class was like getting stabbed by needles in my chest.

If they loved each other, I wanted them to make it clear already.

Personally, I did think I was the one closest to Takamori, and being with him helped me feel at peace. I'd hoped that maybe that feeling could be mutual... And if so, then maybe...

I found an empty park and sat on a bench.

"But I knew this was coming," I told myself again. That very thought, that "then maybe," was proof enough that I actually didn't get it.

I was trying to pressure Fushimi, but I was the one under pressure.

"*It happens to guys, too*," I'd said. "*The boy who likes the protagonist of a girls' manga from the beginning never ends up winning.*"

That was totally right.

I'd liked Takamori from the beginning of high school—until another, more powerful heroine had suddenly appeared to take the *seat beside him* from me.

My own comment sneering at childhood friends had ended up hurting me deeply.

Something pricked at the back of my nose, while the inside of my mouth became hotter and hotter. My vision started turning blurry. The back of my throat tightened as I let out a weak breath.

My head was telling me over and over not to cry, but that voice was fading into silence.

"...I wish I'd realized I loved him sooner."

Even if I'd known this would happen, it still hurt.

"I don't know what I'm gonna say to her...," Fushimi muttered, looking down at her feet.

Torigoe was already gone by the time we got back to the classroom.

Fushimi had told me what had happened—apparently, Torigoe had set us up to make us realize our feelings for each other.

"She mediated for us, but I'm pretty sure she did like you!" Fushimi glanced at me from the side, puffing her cheeks again.

"That doesn't make sense. Why would she do that, then?"

"A girl's heart is more complex than you think."

Is it?

Fushimi and I had just confirmed that we were each other's number one, although I still didn't know whether this was love. The more seriously I thought about it, the more complicated it got.

I'd told Fushimi as much, and she'd said she was fine with that.

"I guess I shouldn't go to the physics room in the meantime."

"Well...hmm... I wonder about that. I feel like still talking with her like normal would be fine, but also I kinda feel like it'd be better to leave her alone..."

"Wow, good thing I've got an expert on girls here to teach me all about them, eh?"

"Hey, we're not a hive mind! I can't know how everyone would feel!"

She actually got mad at that joke.

I hadn't given Torigoe a direct answer, but I guessed she'd come to a conclusion. I mean, pretty hard not to when the boy you confessed to immediately runs after another girl…

She was probably super frustrated with me.

Although, she was the one who'd told me to go after Fushimi…

"Ah, then how about we go for a nice middle ground? Instead of just the two of us…you join us, too."

"W-would that be okay…? I don't know what to think anymore."

Guess our only option is to ask her directly. I took out my phone and started typing the message.

"Ryou, what are you doing?"

"I'm asking Torigoe what she wants."

"Wait, you insensitive jerk! How can you not realize that—?" Fushimi started hitting me, fuming.

The reply arrived instantly.

I want us to act like normal.

"…Guess that's it."

"…I—I see. Well, if that's what she wants."

Then I got another message.

I still want to hang out with Fushimi.

"There you have it."

"T-Torigoe…!" Fushimi got teary-eyed reading the message on my phone's screen.

"Good thing you'll still be friends."

"Yeah."

Fushimi said it might be awkward to go to the physics room the day after this whole mess, so she decided to wait a week or so for things to calm down.

"I'll bring over tons of my novel recs for when we're back!"

She started talking to herself about which ones to take, counting them off on her fingers.

I walked her home, then went back to my house and called Torigoe to thank her for what she did for us.

"Hey."

"What?"

"I'm sorry about all the trouble you went through. And I wanted to thank you."

"It's fine. I couldn't stand watching you both. I just gave you a little push."

Fushimi had said Torigoe actually did like me, but her voice sounded like normal now.

Maybe the whole thing really was an act to encourage us.

"So you're dating now?"

"Hmm? No...not yet..."

"...*What the hell is Fushimi doing?*"

"Huh? You're blaming Fushimi? Not me?"

"Why does she think I did all this? She better not be thinking she's okay now just because you're a stupid loner with a head full of rocks..."

"And now you're insulting me."

"She's never told you she likes you?"

Of course not... Wait.

Back when we skipped school for the beach...? Did she mean...me?

"Sounds like something came to mind, huh? You absolute dumbass."

"Wait a second—don't you think that's a little harsh, Torigoe?"

"It's just the right amount of harsh. And I have every right to be."

Why?

"Fushimi's keeping a promise we made when we were little... She really cares about doing things right, so I think she just feels bound by that..."

"Do you have any idea how much energy it takes to tell someone you like them? Who cares about some promise? Her love is not something that shallow, I'm pretty sure."

Really?

All this time, I'd believed there was no way the prettiest girl at school would be in love with me, and any indication to the contrary was only because she meant to keep her promises, not because she truly liked me.

But if Torigoe was right, I'd been way off the mark.

"If she said anything about any promises, she was using it for cover. I can tell you right now that she loves you for real."

She…loves me…

Hearing it like that made me blush.

F-Fushimi, do you really…?

"Bubby, what're you grinning about?"

"Whaaa—?!" I jumped in surprise and walked backward until I hit the door.

Mana was giving me a weird look.

Right. I'm still in the doorway.

"N-nothing!"

"Really?"

I could hear Torigoe laughing over the phone. She must've heard and pictured what had just happened.

I snatched up my bag and rushed to my room.

Once Torigoe finished cackling, I went over what Fushimi and I had talked about regarding lunchtime, then hung up.

One week later, Fushimi was ready to see her again, and we class reps went over to Torigoe's desk.

"Hey, Torigoe, let's go to the physics room."

"Huh? Ah, yeah."

Torigoe seemed surprised for a moment, but once she saw me grinning behind Fushimi, she accepted with an awkward smile. "…Thanks for inviting me," she said, and Fushimi giggled.

She had a paper bag in her hand. I'd asked her about it that morning, and she'd said it was her top twenty novels. She'd very seriously stated they were her ultra, definitive, Hina-approved seal-of-quality favorites.

She was extremely confident in her choices and planned on gifting them to Torigoe.

"What's that?" Torigoe asked, pointing at the bag.

Fushimi couldn't hold it in anymore and burst with passion to present them to her: "It's the Hina Fushimi Selection! My handpicked top twenty!"

"Nice. You can tell a lot about a person by their top twenty."

"Yesssss!"

Fushimi was over the moon with excitement. In her eyes, I saw her approval (*"You really are a woman of culture"*), to which Torigoe silently nodded (*"Oh, yes. I get you, sister"*).

"Fushimi, I already have this one."

"A-an overlap! I see you have taste!"

"We both do."

They kept praising each other whenever one of them already owned or had read a book the other recommended.

Between Torigoe's calm and Fushimi's energy, they complemented each other quite well, like yin and yang.

Then I realized they were going to leave me in the dust while we were hanging out.

Oh well. At least they're having fun.

They talked with an enthusiasm they never showed our other classmates.

"...I really made the right choice," Torigoe muttered, just loud enough for me to hear.

The smile she gave then is etched in my memory.

"Does Takamori read any books?" Torigoe asked me after Ryou had left to go to the bathroom.

"Y'know… I wonder…" I didn't have many memories of seeing him reading. I had a hard time imagining it. "Why do you ask?"

"He's really dense, don't you think? Like, dangerously so."

"He really is."

"So I was thinking maybe he should read something to better understand a girl's heart."

"Oh, that sounds good!"

Were there any about childhood friends? I was searching all through my mind, when Torigoe named a suggestion.

"That one is really good at showing how a girl feels when her affections aren't returned. It'd be a great reference."

"Mmm…but that one…" I shot her a glare of suspicion.

"What?"

She probably didn't mean anything by recommending that one, since she only tilted her head at my reaction.

"That's the one where the protagonist starts dating his plain classmate and gets her pregnant, isn't it?"

It was a work of Literature, with a capital *L*. The way it depicted the characters of that age and different forms of love was fantastic—I was well aware of how good it was as a story.

But…it had some very intense scenes…particularly the one that took place in bed.

"…" Torigoe immediately looked away.

Oh, you did totally mean it, I see. She's trying to put weird ideas into his head through his reading!

"Is it?"

And now she's playing dumb?!

I loudly cleared my throat. "I think it's a great idea to use books for teaching him, but I don't appreciate the roundabout way of trying to get some ideas into his subconscious."

"What do you mean?"

Stop fooling around!

"Besides, I can't picture him reading a novel."

"Hey, maybe he'll get really into them. I'll give him a little present to whet his interest."

"No! Stop trying to get Ryou to read that pornographic novel!"

"Oh my. You think that masterpiece is pornographic?"

I know… I understand. I know it's a masterpiece. When you take out the sex scene.

She shot me a snobbish stare, as if I was some uncultured swine unable to appreciate true art.

What got me about it, besides that one scene, was the part about the protagonist having an encounter with the class's plain girl and getting her pregnant.

"There's too much overlap!"

"Fushimi, you're not Takamori's mom. I should be able to recommend whatever I want to him."

"You're right, but…"

She was totally choosing a story that could reflect her and Ryou's relationship. The worst part was that it *would* technically help him understand girls, so objecting was hard.

"I doubt he'd read it even if you asked him to anyway." I gave up.

*   *   *

A few days later, the topic came up during our morning walk to school.

"Oh, that. Yeah, Torigoe told me it was good, so I borrowed it."

"You did?"

It really was good, so I couldn't say anything against it.

Ryou took out the thin book from his bag and leafed through the 150-page-long paperback.

"Did you read it?"

"Yup. All of it."

Really...?

"But it had so many complicated words that I understood none of it."

"Really?! I see, I see!"

"...Why are you happy about that?"

"Oh, nothing. I guess it was too soon for you!"

"Hey, what do you mean by that?" he grumpily objected.

I'll get him a manga with a super cute and devoted childhood friend instead.

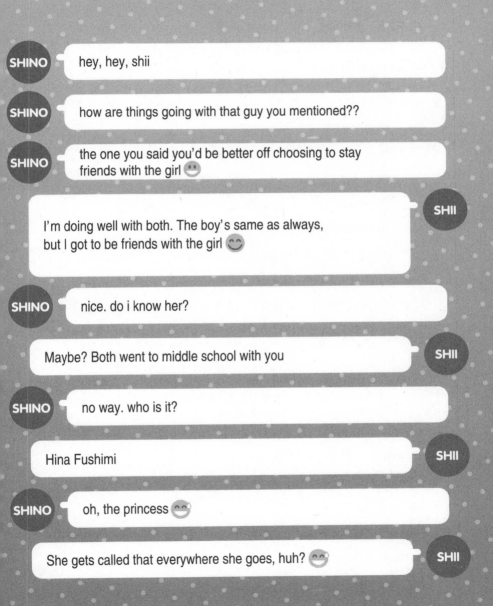

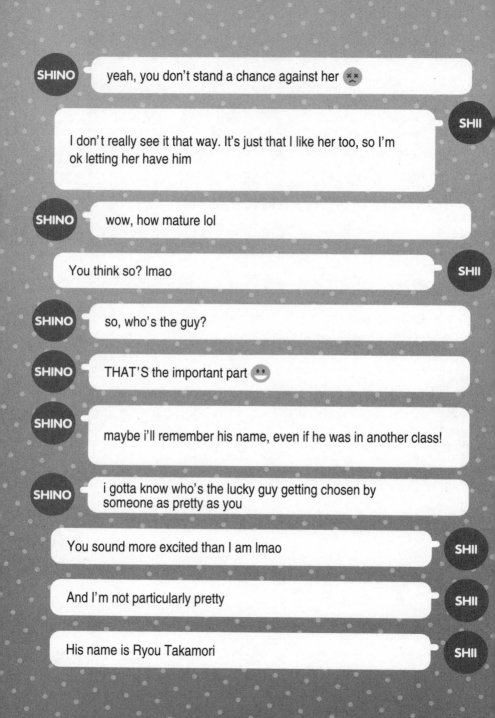

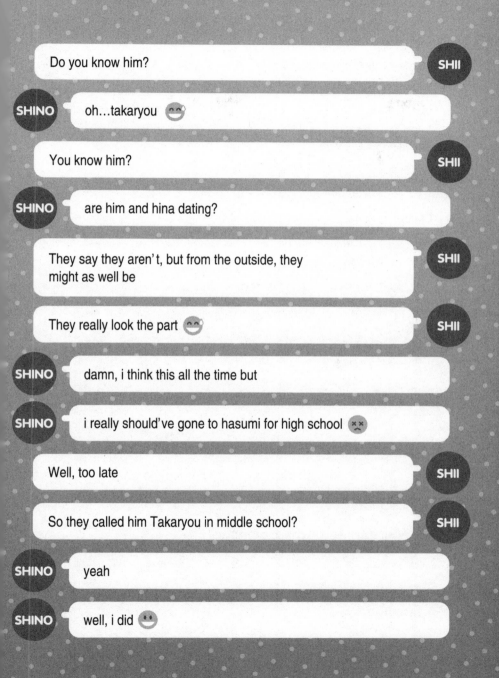

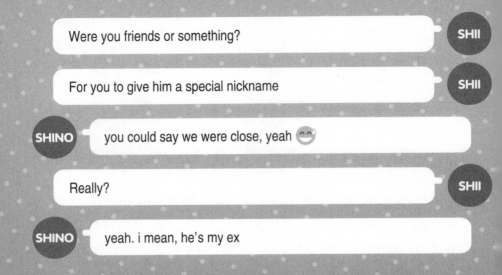

Afterword

Nice to meet you—I'm Kennoji.

This is my second romantic comedy, after *I Time Traveled to My Second Year of High School to Ask Out the Teacher I Liked Back Then*, brought to you once again by GA Bunko.

It's been a year since I last published a new series, and this always makes me antsy. Sometimes I even lose sleep over it.

My previous series was a very sweet and mellow romance, about 90 percent lovey-dovey content for a quite diabetes-inducing experience, but this series is something closer to more traditional romantic fiction. They're both quite different, even if they belong to the same rom-com genre, so please take a look at *Time Travel* if you're interested.

I've also written some isekai fantasies, such as the following:

- *Hazure Skill: The Guild Member with a Worthless Skill Is Actually a Legendary Assassin*
- *Drugstore in Another World: The Slow Life of a Cheat Pharmacist*

And more.

Both of the series above are very fun, so if you're interested in reading my isekai work, please do. The reception of both has been great!

*   *   *

Many people once again helped me in the production of this book. It is all thanks to them that I'm able to get published as an author, so I want to say my thanks.

Hopefully this sells! I pray that this work can bring happiness to all readers and to all staff involved in its production and sale.

I want to thank you all for reading my book.

I hope to see you again next time.